FLYNN'S WORLD

FLYNN'S WORLD

Gregory Mcdonald

PANTHEON BOOKS

NEW YORK

All rights reserved under International and Pan-American Copyright
Conventions. Published in the United States by Pantheon Books,
a division of Random House, Inc., New York, and simultaneously in
Canada by Random House of Canada Limited, Toronto.

Pantheon Books and colophon are registered trademarks of
Random House, Inc.

Library of Congress Cataloging-in-Publication Data

Mcdonald, Gregory, 1937–
Flynn's world / Gregory Mcdonald.
p.   cm.
ISBN 0-375-42236-6
1. Flynn, Francis Xavier (Fictitious character)—Fiction.
2. College teachers—Crimes against—Fiction. 3. Police—
Massachusetts—Boston—Fiction. 4. Boston (Mass.)—Fiction.
I. Title.

PS3563.A278 F52 2003   813'.54—dc21   2002192601

www.pantheonbooks.com

Book design by M. Kristen Bearse

Printed in the United States of America
First Edition
2   4   6   8   9   7   5   3   1

If chaos is to be avoided,
probably it is necessary to assume
that we are coming from somewhere, and,
to presume that we are going somewhere.

— GREGORY MCDONALD

FLYNN'S WORLD

ONE

—◆—

"Da! Da! Wake up!"

In his sleep, Boston Police Inspector Francis Xavier Flynn again was on the ground, a boy asleep against a warm brick wall. The other side of that wall, a city was burning.

"Da! Wake up!"

Cross-legged, his thirteen-year-old daughter, Jenny, sat on the rug beside his bed. Bathed in the light that came through the opened bedroom door, her curly blond hair gleamed; her brilliant blue eyes, as big as saucers, beamed at him.

"Why are you waking me up in the middle of the night?" He felt for Elsbeth. She was not in the bed with him.

"It's not the middle of the night, Da. It's only eight-fifteen."

"Right. I came to bed at six o'clock, didn't I? Having had no sleep at all last night." He had spent Saturday, Saturday night until four-thirty Sunday afternoon discovering the whereabouts of a woman who had taken a car from outside a pharmacy. The car was not hers. In a safety seat in the back of the car was a sixteen-month-old girl. The baby was not hers, either.

Flynn turned on his bedside lamp. He said to Jenny, "The question remains. Why is my bit of fluff awakening me in the middle of my night?"

On the rug between her knees were a hammer, a screwdriver, a pair of pliers, a flashlight, a box of gauze, and a bottle of tincture of iodine.

"Need you. Please get dressed and come with me." Without using her hands or arms, she stood up from where she had been sitting cross-legged. "As quick as you possibly ever can."

"Where are we going?" he asked.

"Cemetery."

"But I'm not dead yet, I don't think."

She picked up the odd collection of things from the floor. "Please hurry. I'll make you a cup of Red Zinger tea while you're getting dressed."

———

"Oof!" In the cemetery Flynn fell into a hole in the ground filled with dead leaves. "Oh, me God." He rolled over in the leaves and sat up. "For an instant there, I thought the grave had reached up and pulled me down. And before my fill of formaldehyde, too!"

After climbing over the cemetery's stone wall Flynn had followed his daughter up a hill thick with dead leaves. In the fog the tombstones were not at all visible at a distance; when they did loom into view they appeared bigger than they were. There was full moonlight in the low fog. Jenny had rushed on ahead without using her flashlight.

Holding his hand, Jenny had hurried him down the steps of their house and along the foggy Winthrop sidewalk.

"What's all this about?" Flynn had asked.

"Billy."

"What's a Billy?" Part of Flynn's mind was still in the bed, asleep. "A billy's a goat. Or a nightstick."

"Billy's my friend."

"Oh, I see. Of the male variety?"

"He's a boy."

"How do we know Billy, although I'm not sure I do?"

"He's been to the house." A goodly number of children wandered through Flynn's house, as he had five of his own. He could not swear to have studied them all. He doubted he had ever seen the faces of some—those who seemed to stand permanently facing the inside of the opened refrigerator.

"Is Billy at school with you?"

"He goes to public school."

"Is he in trouble?"

"He's in the cemetery."

"Dead or alive is he?"

"Discomfited," she said with dignity.

"Then he must be alive."

"Sometimes Billy and I meet in the cemetery. You know, to talk things over. Religion. Politics. Billy loves history."

"Why on earth do you meet in the cemetery?"

"It's quiet there."

"I expect it is."

"Sometimes we take the names and dates from the tombstones and imagine what the people, families must have been like when they were alive, you know? Billy and I make up stories about them."

"You meet this boy in the cemetery after dark?"

"Sometimes. Billy's not afraid of things like that. I know some people are."

"Not you, though."

"Besides, Billy's on the wrestling team. He says he's not ready yet for all the guys, you know, to josh him about seeing so much of me. A girl."

"I see."

"Who'd believe that Billy and I just meet and talk? Mostly . . ."

"Who indeed? Especially after dark in a cemetery? I admit to a small degree of incredulity myself, Ms. Fluff."

"Here's the place in the wall we climb over."

"Where's the main gate?"

"Oh, that's way down the road. It's locked after dark, anyway."

"Ah, yes." Flynn lifted one tweed leg over the low stone wall. "I've heard people are dyin' to get into this cemetery."

By the time he fell she had disappeared uphill in the fog.

Returning down the hill, Jenny flashed the light on her father sitting on dead leaves. "Why are you sitting there? We're in a hurry."

"I'm resting," he said. "In the last forty-eight hours I've had two hours of sleep, I remind you. If you had asked me at five o'clock this afternoon how I envisioned myself spending the night, I doubt I would have said dashing about after you among tombstones in a fog."

"Oh, yeah." Jenny turned off the flashlight. "Did you find the woman and the baby?"

"I found the woman," Flynn said. "Then I found the baby. Would you believe the woman had hidden the baby in a clothes drier?"

"Sixteen-month-old baby." Jenny sniffed. Much had been expected of the Flynn children. "Ought to be able to make noise. Walk."

"Indeed, yes," agreed Flynn. "As well as fold her own diapers. The baby was peacefully, soundly asleep in the drier, which I would very much like to be at this very moment, myself."

"In a clothes drier?"

"Anywhere!"

"How did you find her? I mean, the baby?"

"By telling the woman we weren't going to look for her. See? There's good in us all, if you can just believe it."

Jenny looked up the hill. "Billy still needs rescuing."

"Jenny, I doubt Billy's falling into a hole or whatever is a police matter."

"May be."

"Are you sure you want someone of my august police rank involved in whatever foolishness Billy has gotten himself into?"

"Why not?"

"I mean, why did you raise me from the nearly dead to come help you extricate your friend Billy from his discomfit in a cemetery?"

"What do you mean?"

"Why didn't you enlist the help of your brothers, Randy and Todd, who, at age fifteen, have already shown considerable resourcefulness in matters delicate and in?"

"Oh, Da." Jenny's voice dropped. "You know they're at the makeup basketball game."

"Sunday night? Oh, yes. I guess I forgot that." Flynn stood up from his mulch pile. "All right, then. If I'm Billy's only hope, lead on, MacFluff."

More slowly this time, Jenny led her father up the cemetery's hill.

"I must say," Flynn said, "you seem to have an uncommon working knowledge of this boneyard. After dark, and in the fog, too. Prior to this, I've only visited this particular piece of real estate socially."

Jenny said, "Me, too."

———

"Ah, well, lad: someone doesn't approve of you all that much."

Standing as tall as he could in the foggy graveyard, Billy's head was close against a tree.

His right ear had been nailed to the tree.

"Who did this to you?"

Billy said nothing.

"That's the way of it, is it?" With the flashlight, Flynn examined the carpentry closely. "Whoever did this to you did you no favors at all. That nail has a sizable head on it. And he nailed you flush to the tree. And you're not saying who did this to you?"

Billy said nothing.

Flynn handed the flashlight back to Jenny. He sat on the ground a couple of meters from the boy and the tree.

Jenny stood between them, looking back and forth from one to the other.

Flynn rested his back against a tombstone.

Silently, he proceeded to pack his pipe.

Jenny said, "Da? Aren't you going to do anything?"

"Anything what?"

"Anything about Billy?"

"I am doing something. I'm scanning my vast intellect, searching for a possible answer to the question I just asked your friend."

"Da, we must get Billy unstuck. He's been standing here two hours!"

"Has he, indeed."

Billy said, "Mr. Flynn? Pretty soon, I've got to pee, you know."

"Yes," Flynn said sympathetically. "In life, we all must face the inevitable."

Jenny asked, "Does your ear hurt, Billy?"

"Not if I stand still."

A well-built boy standing so still against a tree reminded Flynn of a sleeping horse.

Flynn asked, "Are you a member of a gang, Billy?"

"No, sir."

"Never have been?"

"No, sir."

Flynn lit his pipe. It was good seeing the flare of his kitchen match in the foggy, dark, cold cemetery. "Billy, you have displeased someone. That's the real problem to be solved. Before I get you unhinged from the tree, I would like to know whom you have displeased, and how."

Billy said nothing.

From the ground, Flynn looked up the half-grown oak tree. "And it's a fine, sturdy tree, isn't it? I daresay it will live another one hundred years or more. It won't even notice your ear is nailed to it. When your flesh begins to rot, your skeleton will drop to the ground. Probably the local household dogs will bury your bones for you."

Eyes visibly huge even in the dark, in the fog, Jenny said, "Da!"

"You see, Billy, someone wants you to make a decision, while you're standing there; prove something of yourself. Jenny said you love to read history. Are you aware of the history of what has happened to you?"

"No, sir."

"But you'd like to know, wouldn't you?"

"No, sir. Not really. Not under the circumstances."

"But how are we to solve this particular mystery unless we review all relevant facts concerning it?"

"What mystery?" the boy asked.

"How we happened to find you standing upright against a stout tree, your ear nailed to it, after dark in a cemetery? For example, did anyone know you were meeting Jenny here tonight?"

"No, sir. Just Jenny."

"Then someone must have followed you here. And that someone did not expect you to be so quickly found, at least not until daylight, perhaps not until the demise and slow funeral of one of our citizens, which could be days hence." Flynn's hand scruffed the dead leaves beside him. "Sure, there's no gardening going on in this particular cemetery this dead season."

"Da." Except for the pliers, Jenny put her odd collection on the ground. "I'll free Billy myself."

"You're not a tree surgeon," Flynn said. "From your choice of implements, I'd say you have a dim future in any branch of surgery."

"I'll do it."

"Mr. Flynn?"

"Yes, Billy?"

"I'm afraid I'm going to sneeze."

"It might solve your problem," Flynn said.

"That's what I'm afraid of."

"In the days of yore . . ." Flynn relit his pipe so he could enjoy the flare of the match. ". . . which was just after Once upon a time, Jenny, darling—"

Jenny expostulated, "Da, this is no time for a witty history lesson! I'm sorry I told you Billy likes history. Are you going to help Billy, or not?"

"I am helping him—when a miscreant displeased his fellow citizens, they sometimes would nail his ear to a tree, usually on the town square, usually on market day. This, of course, shamed the miscreant, a punitive device not much in vogue in these days of relentless understanding. The villagers would watch him. He'd be further shamed as he discovered no neighbors, friends, or relatives would do a thing to free him from the tree. Everyone would be waiting, you see, to see how long the miscreant would stand there in his public mortification and isolation before taking matters into his own ear, you might say, and rip his ear from the tree. I daresay a certain amount of wagering went on, with perhaps eyes on the clock. Or, I expect in some instances, calendar. By the end of this exercise in justice, not only would the miscreant be punished, for whatever he had done to displease his fellows, something of the miscreant's true character would have been revealed, to himself, and all others."

"Da! Is this true?"

"True as I'm sittin' here on the cold cemetery ground on a foggy night, my back resting not too comfortably against a tombstone, wishin' I were at home in my own wee bed hammerin' a pillow."

"Billy, what did you do?" Jenny asked.

"And to whom?"

"Okay," Billy said. "Leave me alone. I'll take care of it. I'll do it. Just not in front of you." The boy's voice deepened. "Thanks for trying to help, Jenny. Thanks for coming, Mr. Flynn. Now just please go away. Both of you."

"But your ear!"

"My ear's my business," Billy said.

"How much longer do you think you'll stand there?" Flynn asked.

"Not long. Now that I understand. I'll do it as soon as you're gone."

"Tear your ear from the tree, Billy?" Jenny was horrified.

Flynn put his cold pipe in his coat pocket. He stood up.

Jenny watched her father pick up the hammer, screwdriver, flashlight.

"Here, Jenny. You hold the light. Steady, now. I'm sleep deprived. Never was all that good at carpentry anyway. Remember the time, Jenny, I hung the closet door upside down?"

Flynn began to chisel the wood behind Billy's ear.

Billy asked, "Mr. Flynn, why did you decide to help me, after all you said?"

"Because I believed you would rip your ear from the tree soon after we were gone. You didn't offer me any lies as to who did this to you, and why. Hush, now. I'm concentratin'. I don't want to hurt the tree any more than I need to."

After chiseling the wood away from all sides of the nail, Flynn slid Billy's ear along its shaft, closer to the tree. With the pliers he then relieved the tree and Billy's ear of the nail.

Billy sneezed.

"Ah!" Flynn said. "Jenny, we weren't a moment too soon!"

———

Alone, Flynn staggered through the front door of his house.

In the front hall, Elsbeth was just taking off her coat.

"I thought you were home hours ago," she said.

"So did I." He started up the stairs.

"The twins won the basketball game."

"All by themselves?"

"Did you get your messages? Sergeant Whelan called, sounding quite cheery. First he said to remind you you must be in court at nine in the morning. I forget which case. He stressed it was Courtroom 9. He won't be picking you up in the morning. And he said you have a meeting with Captain Walsh at two-thirty. You're to be fired. Apparently he called again, and gave the same message to Todd: you're to be fired tomorrow. It's past ten and I don't know where Jenny is."

Without turning around at the top of the stairs, Flynn said, "She's been with me. I left her in the boneyard, I suspect discussing inevitability with a friend."

"Oh, and Frannie?" Elsbeth called up the stairs. "The President of Harvard University called. He'd like you to call him back."

"Sure." Flynn closed the door to his dark bedroom. "Call the President of Harvard. Sure, sure, sure. Right away next week."

T W O

—◆—

"Now, Da. Listen." On the front seat of the car, close beside Flynn, Winny settled his schoolbooks on his lap.

"When have I ever not listened?" Flynn asked. "More's the pity."

"You see those six birds on that tree branch?"

Flynn lowered his head to look up through the windshield. "I do."

"If I shot one of them off, how many would be left on the branch?"

"None."

"None!"

"The others would fly away."

"Oh, Da. Someday I'll make up my own riddle and you won't get it."

"At the age of nine, my son, you already are your own riddle."

A back door of the ancient Country Squire station wagon opened. The "Flynn-twin," as they were commonly known, Randy and Todd, climbed into the car, throwing their sports bags behind their seat.

"Ah, Winny gets the front seat this morning!" With his left hand, Todd messed up Winny's hair.

"Cut that out!" Winny had worked hard on making the part in his long brown hair perfect to his own eyes. "You guys! Da, why don't you beat one of them to death with the other one!"

"I'll consider it," Flynn said.

At fifteen, Todd was slightly more blond than his identical twin, his nose a centimeter shorter. He spoke a little faster, was a little less precise in his violin playing. On the soccer field and basketball court he was also slightly more aggressive than his brother, who would hesitate that fraction of a second and usually make the more dazzling play.

Randy rolled down the car window and shouted at the house. "Jenny! Get your face out of the mirror! There's nothing you can do about your looks! We'll be late for school!"

"Jenny was late getting home last night." Winny was trying to perfect the part in his hair in the rearview mirror.

Behind the steering wheel, Flynn turned his broad shoulders to look at the twins in the backseat.

"Did either of you know Jenny has been meeting with a boy in the cemetery?"

"No," Todd said. "What boy?"

"I did," Randy answered. "Billy."

"Who's Billy?" Todd asked.

"Capriano."

"The wrestler at the high school?"

"Yeah."

"Capriano," Flynn said. "I've seen that name somewhere. Recently."

"He's a neat kid," Randy said.

"What do you know about him?" Flynn asked.

"Not much. Seen him around. Parties. Used to be in Scouts with us. He beat Bobby Wentworth."

"Nobody ever beat Bobby Wentworth," Todd said in defense of the Cartwright School wrestling champion.

"Bill Capriano did."

"I've run into him in the library," Todd said. "He's an altar boy."

"Runs with a tough bunch, does he?" asked Flynn.

"Billy? No."

"A street fighter?"

"No way. He's smart."

Flynn addressed Randy. "You object to his meeting Jenny in the graveyard?"

Randy shrugged. "Her business."

"Did you know they were meeting last night?"

"Not particularly."

"Yes or no?"

"No. But she didn't come to our basketball game. So I guessed."

"How did you know they meet?"

"I saw Jenny climbing over the cemetery wall one afternoon. Billy was inside the cemetery, between the trees."

"What did you do about that?"

"I waved at him. Billy's a nice kid, Da. I trust him with my little sister, okay?"

"Is there something you want us to do about this?" Todd asked.

Jenny was coming down the back steps of the house. A hair drier, cord dangling, was on top of the books cradled in her arms.

"Yes," Flynn said. "The next time I ask you about Billy Capriano, which I expect will be soon, I'd like you to know more about him."

Jenny got into the front seat beside Winny. "Who put my hair drier in the laundry basket?"

Flynn started the car.

He readjusted the rearview mirror.

The routine: Todd said, "Randy did"; Randy said, "Winny did"; Winny said, "Jeff did."

"Sure. At ten months old, Jeff put my hair drier in the laundry basket."

"Boy oh boy," Winny said. "I'm glad that kid was born. It was tough bein' the youngest in the family all these years."

Flynn turned left out of his driveway toward Cartwright School.

Todd muttered, "If you hadn't spent all night talkin' to the other witches in the cemetery with Billy Capriano"—he said the name loudly—"you would have been up in time to find your hair drier."

"Da! Did you tell them?"

"Not everything."

"Everything what?" asked Winny. "Did something grave happen in the cemetery?"

Flynn looked down at his nine-year-old son.

"It's not funny." Jenny made a double-defensive turn in the conversation. "I have to use the hair drier after swimming practice. You think it's nice coming out in this weather with a wet head?"

Autumn weather: all three of Flynn's sons continued to wear their school-uniform shorts.

"I don't use your damned hair drier," Todd muttered.

"I use a towel, myself," Randy said. "Saves electricity."

Winny said nothing.

"Maybe if you didn't use an electric hair drier," Randy continued, "your hair wouldn't be so damned bumpy."

"It's called 'curly,'" Jenny said. "Da likes it that way."

"What about Billy Capriano?" Randy said. "How does he like your hair?"

"In his mouth," Todd said.

Flynn looked at Todd through the rearview mirror.

Todd jumped forward. He folded his arms across the back of the front seat. "If you get fired today, Da, can we go back to Loch Nafooie?"

"How did you know I'm going to get fired today?"

"Grover left that message with me yesterday. He made a special point of telling me. He said, 'Be sure and tell your father Captain Walsh is going to fire him tomorrow afternoon.' I don't think Grover likes me much."

Randy laughed. "Not since that time we beat the lights out of him on a Cambridge sidewalk."

Winny sang, "Da's gonna get fired / Da's gonna get fired."

"Sergeant Richard T. Whelan takes his job very seriously." Flynn turned the car into the Cartwright School's driveway. "Which does him no good at all at all."

"If we have to go back to the farm on Loch Nafooie," Randy said, "we could ride our horses to school every day."

"Yeah," Jenny added. "You could sleep late in the mornings, Da."

"Sit by the fire and smoke my pipe. Read again the great

Irish writers everyone thinks are English." The children were piling out of the car. "Shoulders back. Ears and eyes open," Flynn advised them. "Mouths closed."

He noticed most of the boys milling about in front of the main school building still wore their uniform shorts. If they were ever ordered to do so in forty-five degree weather, doubtlessly they would complain.

Flynn proceeded toward Boston and Courtroom 9.

He and his family had enjoyed the year he had spent at the farm in Ireland, while waiting for the international intelligence community to accept his death while on assignment in Burundi.

After a year, however, John Roy Priddy, No Name Zero, decided he wanted Francis Xavier Flynn, N. N. 13, more available for the odd intelligence assignment "between the borders," which was where No Name operated.

Thus he had been moved to Boston, Massachusetts, the United States of America, with the cover job of the Boston Police Department's only inspector.

Elsbeth, his wife, a sabra, born and raised in Israel, found both places cold and damp. Somehow she had managed to warm their homes in Ireland and the United States just by the width and depth of her personality, wit, and love.

Flynn nestled the huge, boxy station wagon next to the fire hydrant in front of the courthouse.

"Now to testify against a poor soul who swears his gun fired and accidentally killed his mother-in-law a day after his wife ran off with the postman." Flynn locked his car. "His aim was that bad."

———

"The judge will see you now," the court officer whispered in Flynn's ear. "In chambers."

Flynn had sat patiently in the courtroom, as most employees of police departments learn to do, thinking of ships and shoes and sealing wax, while the wheels of justice ground exceedingly slow, wide men in thin suits milling around the judge's raised desk, muttering madly, slapping this paper after that on the judge's desk ever so much like players of poker.

Until Michael Carruth, shackled, in prison uniform, was brought in for sentencing.

Flynn had then given the court officer a note and asked him to deliver it to the judge immediately.

The note read:

Dear Judge Goldston:
Before uttering sentence upon the miscreant before
you, Michael Carruth, it is imperative you speak to me.
Inspector Francis Flynn

At the door to the judge's chambers, Flynn looked around at the miscreant. He was a small, light-boned, black person.

His eyes were blazing at Flynn.

First his lips mouthed at Flynn, "No, no."

Then he stood up and shouted, "No, Flynn, you bastard! Don't do it! Stop!"

In chambers, Judge Goldston said, "I was wondering

what you're doing in my courtroom this morning, Frank. I don't have anything coming up in which you're involved."

"You don't?"

"No, sir."

"You're not hearing *The Commonwealth v. Oral McMahon*?"

The judge consulted some papers on his desk. "Jack has that. In Courtroom 6. Someone gave you a bum steer."

"Someone did." GROVER!

"Sit down." The judge did so. "Want some coffee?"

"I never take stimulants." Flynn sat. "I find life quite exciting enough."

The judge chuckled. "How about sedatives?"

"I fall asleep every time I think of trying one."

"How's Elsbeth?"

"Dandy."

"I want you to know that musicale you and Elsbeth and the kids put on at our shul last spring was the high point of our year."

"Elsbeth talked us into that. She said what good is it to play ensemble only for our own pleasure." Flynn smiled. "Did you mind the Spanish piece in praise of St. James at all?"

"I liked it."

"St. James praised in shul. I expect he enjoyed that."

"So?" Judge Goldston laughed. "Last year the temple gave me a testimonial. And I'm no saint!"

"Who among us is?"

"That Jenny. Was there ever a more beautiful child?"

"No."

"What's this about Carruth?"

"You're about to sentence him, I overheard, for three counts of rape."

"Yes."

"Did the women identify him?"

"Nope. Every incident took place in the dark of an alley. He wore a ski mask."

"Was his semen matched to that found in the women?"

Judge Goldston was scanning his papers. "It doesn't exactly say so here."

"But the raped women were semen stained?"

"Yes. The man confessed, Frank. Lieutenant Detective John Kurt—you know him?"

"No."

"Astonishing conviction record. Truly astonishing. Kurt did the interrogation. Carruth was sent for ten days' psychiatric evaluation. The docs are convinced Carruth is our man. He told all, in graphic detail, fit all the psychological patterns of a serial rapist, expressed no remorse. A plea of guilty was accepted seven weeks ago. What's the problem?"

"I wouldn't say he's exactly innocent," Flynn said. "But he didn't do it."

"How do you know?"

"Met him professionally about a year ago. Five times he was beaten up on the streets of our fair city for soliciting males. Finally I convinced him he had very little future in carryin' on as he was."

"Still, a rapist of females—"

"Carruth is incapable of producing semen. Further, due to botched surgery, even if he could produce semen he is

23

incapable of transmitting it, you might say, to another human being. The docs didn't notice?"

"Yee, gods."

"I think Carruth wants the world to think him better, in a certain way, than he is."

"He wants to go to prison?"

"He wants to go to a male prison."

"You're sure of this?"

"You'll have to check, of course. Until then, I strongly suggest you delay sentencing."

"You're saving the taxpayers some money, again, 'Reluctant' Flynn."

At the door to chambers, Flynn said, "More to the point, there's a cad out there who is a rapist, free to rape again. You might suggest to Lieutenant Detective John Kurt that next time you'll be more impressed by his thoroughness than his 'astounding' arrest record."

Leaving the judge's chambers, Flynn focused on the man at the prosecutor's table who obviously was Lt. Kurt.

The unsmiling man looked at Flynn with steady blue eyes.

From the defense table, the defendant, due to be freed, shouted, "Flynn, you prick! I hate you, hate you!"

"Och, man," Flynn said back to the man. "Aren't you in enough of a prison as it is?"

THREE

———◆———

"Cocky left a message for me to call you," Flynn said to his wife over his desk phone.

After dropping in at Courtroom 6 and being told *The Commonwealth v. McMahon* had been continued for the ninth time, Flynn treated himself to a leisurely lunch at Jacob Wirth's before proceeding to his office on the third floor of the Old Records Building on Craigie Lane. The German cuisine reminded Flynn of the best of his youth in Germany.

"You forgot I have to bring Jeff in for his checkup this afternoon?" Elsbeth asked.

"Change his oil and grease him, or a full tune-up?"

"You forgot to give me the money for the doctor's appointment?"

"How much is it?"

"A week's wages, Frannie. Plus to remind you that's where I'll be all afternoon. Despite our having a fixed appointment, the doctor will make me wait at least three hours to prove to me how valuable his time is while Jeff and

I pick up every infection, staph and otherwise, in his crowded waiting room."

"Elsbeth, are you sure these monthly appointments are really necessary? The lad is as strong as goat cheese."

"What if something went wrong with the baby, Frannie? We'd have only ourselves to blame."

"Would we? The doctors prescribe guilt, is that it?"

"Did you leave some money in the house?"

Although they collected receipts and kept good records, the Flynns paid cash for nearly everything.

"In my boot," Flynn said. "My left hiking boot."

Dragging his left leg behind him, carrying the small tray in only his right hand, Cocky entered Flynn's office.

"Ah," Flynn informed his wife. "Here's Cocky now with a nice cuppa."

"Give him my best."

Taking his mug of herb tea from the tray Cocky had placed on his desk, Flynn said to her, "While I have you on the horn, old dear . . . does the name Capriano mean anything to you?"

"They're our butchers, Frannie."

"Are they indeed?"

"You don't know the name of our butchers?"

"How many of them are there?"

"Two brothers. Tony and William. You've been in the shop a hundred times."

"Tony and William! Yes. Their last name is Capriano?"

"They have a big sign over their door. It says CAPRIANOS' MEATS."

"Do they indeed? Anything else odd about them?"

"William has a finger missing."

"Many a butcher does. Occupational hazard. He didn't sell it to us, did he, along with the week's sausage order?"

"He lost it while serving in the Marines, Frannie. Someone slammed a jeep's door on it, or something."

"I'm looking for dirt, old thing. Rumors of drink, drugs, gambling, violence, wife abuse . . . ?"

"They're wonderful people. I know their wives, their children, most of them, at least by sight, very polite, helpful."

"You know Billy? Is he William's son?"

"Yes."

"What do you know about Billy?"

"Jenny is stuck on him. Billy is stuck on Jenny. They're just four big eyes, two blue, two brown, eating each other up. Frannie, I think they're having first love with each other. How nice."

"Jenny is too young for that."

"Frannie, you still think I'm too young for that."

"You are. Who are you stuck on now?"

"Still my first love."

"Still? What, against progress, are you? You'll never see yourself on daytime television that way."

"I keep looking for someone else, but what to do? Every other man I meet is a bore."

"Me, too. So how do you know about Jenny and Billy? I was about to tell you their secret."

"You were about to tell me the secret that they meet alone in the cemetery?"

"I thought I was half up on things."

"You do very well, for a busy father of five."

"Thank you. How did you first find out about Billy?"

"Joan of Arc."

"I see. Joan of Arc told you. You women do stick together."

"All of a sudden, Jenny knew everything about Joan of Arc. Then Henry the Eighth. And each of his wives. Helping me peel potatoes one Sunday she told me the whole history of the Peloponnesian War, as if I'd asked. Sparta won, by the way."

"Yeah, but it took them nearly thirty years."

"Twenty-seven. When Jenny got Todd into a half nelson he couldn't break free of I knew there had to be a Billy somewhere."

"A wrestler who loves to read history."

"Every good mother is a detective, Inspector Flynn."

"But not, surely, every good wife?"

"So who put Jenny's hair drier in the laundry basket this morning?"

"I did." Flynn laughed. "She'd left it in the sink. Actually, I just left it on the top of the hamper. It must have fallen in."

"Every good wife, too," Elsbeth said.

"You couldn't even find the money for the doctor."

"I hadn't even looked yet. I just wanted to talk to you a few moments without the sweet music of the Flynn household."

Flynn reviewed the sweet music of the Flynn household: scraping violins to the accompaniment of a bouncing basketball, a mewling baby, various arias to the theme of "Where's my shirt?" "Who took my book?" . . .

In the alcove near the fireplace, Cocky studied the chess-board.

"But where have I seen the name Capriano lately?" Flynn mused.

"In letters a meter high across the top of their storefront maybe?"

"No. Someplace odder than that."

"If they sent you a bill, we've paid already. I have to get Jeff ready to go wait in the doctor's office so he can catch a staph infection the doctor can charge us for."

"Be sure and look in the right boot for the money," Flynn said. "The other boot has a live mousetrap in it."

"You said the left boot. The money is in the left boot, you said."

Flynn said, "The left boot is the right boot."

He hung up.

His tea was still warm.

"How's your cold?" he asked Cocky.

The weekend before, Cocky had found himself inade-quately dressed and shod in the mountain snows of the Rod and Gun Club in western New England.

As a detective and as a man he had been more than ade-quate.

He had been heroic.

"Much better."

Tea in hand, Flynn approached the chessboard. "Are you acquainted with a Lieutenant Detective John Kurt?"

"Arrogant bastard. Cock-of-the-walk type. Is there a problem?"

"Maybe. But your eyes still seem peculiarly bright this afternoon, Cocky. Glassy, I'd almost say."

"I had to go to a bank this morning." Cocky grinned up at Flynn.

"Such an excursion has been known to open many a person's eyes. You moved your queen *there*? It's a dastardly diversion!"

"Open a savings account." Cocky watched Flynn to see if he understood.

"I don't know." Flynn fingered his black knight. "What to think."

Lieutenant Detective Walter Concannon, a few years before, while arresting a counterfeiter in the living room of his house, had been shot in the spine by the counterfeiter's nine-year-old son.

Recovered as much as he was going to, Cocky was given early retirement and half pay.

A bachelor, whose passion was chess and whose genius was research, he attached himself to Flynn. Flynn never asked him, but he suspected Cocky had set himself up in a room somewhere in the vast, nearly empty Old Records Building, with a cot, hot plate, refrigerator within, a necessarium somewhere nearby.

Flynn knew Cocky seldom left the building. He was there, day and night, including weekends, whenever Flynn called. Never had he accepted an invitation to Flynn's home. His agreeing to go with Flynn to the Rod and Gun Club had been a most welcome surprise.

Cocky's having gone to a bank that morning therefore was news. Diverted by the chess game, Flynn's mind was registering the fact that previously, Cocky had not had a savings account.

"After you left Friday, Frank, I got two checks."

"Is that so?"

"A check for full pay."

"Is that so?"

"My first since the accident." Cocky always referred to his being shot in the spine by a nine-year-old as "an accident." Petey Lipton, the nine-year-old who shot him in the spine, had been institutionalized only a few months. "I guess I'm back on full pay."

"That's good," Flynn said.

"Off the retired list!"

"We never did accept the way the City of Boston threw away your superbly functioning brain with your slightly impaired body, did we?"

"The second check also was from the City of Boston."

"Is that so?"

"For all my back pay!"

"Good God, Cocky! You're rich!"

Cocky laughed. "I've never seen so much money! I spent all weekend staring at the check. Figuring it out. Every penny is there from my being on half pay since the accident! Plus interest!"

"Och, well!" Flynn clapped Cocky on the shoulder. "It's the Fiji Islands for you, isn't it, my man, with a girl in a grass skirt on each knee!"

"Do such girls play chess?"

"They do! Except they spell it with a *T*, I think. Or is it a red sports car for you to cruise the cow paths of Boston while you tootle 'Danny Boy' on the horn?"

"Not that, Flynn. I'd just get elected mayor."

"That you might. Well, don't put much of your new wealth down on this particular game of chess. Even though you've got me as puzzled as the abbot who woke up in the forest next to a yawning abyss."

"Sure, you've got your next three moves all planned, haven't you?"

"To Headquarters I go." Flynn put his topcoat back on. "To be fired summarily by Captain of Police Timothy Walsh. I admit I've spent very little of my life in offices, Lieutenant Walter Concannon, no-longer-Retired, and am therefore somewhat innocent of office politics. But would you say my supposition that office politics is the avocation of the vocationally incompetent approaches the truth?"

"Today," Cocky said, "I'd agree with you, Frank, even if you said the moon is made of our best intentions."

Outside his closed office door, Flynn took only a few steps before turning back and reopening the door. "'The moon is made of our best intentions,'" he quoted. "That's a good line, old Cockerel."

Cocky said, "Been around you too long, Frank."

Flynn took no steps before reopening his office door and sticking his head inside again.

He said, "No. You haven't."

FOUR

"Sit down, Inspector." The eyes of Captain Timothy Walsh were still liquid from his lunch.

Flynn sat in a chair facing the captain's desk.

He had not been surprised, upon entering the office, to find Sergeant Richard T. Whelan, Flynn's own assistant, sitting in a light chair toward the side of the office. He, too, looked a little lunch-flushed. He looked as expectant as a four-year-old on Christmas Eve.

Flynn greatly preferred his ancient Old Records Building to Police Headquarters. Headquarters was all plastic, glass, beige and gray tin, warrens he understood were called work stations, which provided the workers with only the illusion of privacy. The proliferation of police uniforms at Headquarters discomfited Flynn. It made him feel like a fox surrounded by hounds. Computerizing records had left most of the Old Records Building empty. There were a few bright offices on the first floor. Typically the people who worked there darted about in comfortable clothes and oversized eyeglasses, maintaining and running computers, usually to the joyful noises of Mozart or Metallica. Otherwise, vast dusty wooden corridors passed by vast dusty empty rooms. Flynn's office, on the third floor, was huge. A large arched window behind his desk overlooked Boston Harbor. There he had genuine privacy, to nap on the divan, play chess with Cocky in the alcove by the fireplace. If he ever saw a police uniform in the Old Records Building he would assume he was being raided.

"Kind of you to suggest I make a courtesy call upon you," Flynn said to Captain Timothy Walsh. "I admit I'm not very astute at performing these relationship duties apparently so crucial to the smooth running of all enterprises American."

Captain Walsh glanced at Sergeant Whelan. "You're not American, are you, Flynn?"

"Neither born nor brought up here, to my grief. But I do my best to muddle along."

"Your best doesn't appear to be good enough." Captain Walsh shifted catarrh in his throat. "Tell me, Frank: how are you?"

"Better than you, apparently."

"How's your appendix?"

"I haven't heard from it lately."

"Could that be because you've had it removed twice? These records indicate you've had two leaves of absence to have your appendix removed."

"It keeps growing back," Flynn said. "I'm that healthy."

"Several prolonged absences for colitis. Five separate absences to bury your mother. Etc. Did you have five mothers?" In fact, Flynn's mother, and father, had been shot to death in their kitchen, executed, when Flynn was fourteen. He had discovered their bodies upon returning home from school. He had never known if, when, where they were buried. "How many more mothers do you have?"

"You're very kind to express such interest in my personal health and life," Flynn said. "How's your own mother?"

"She's well," said Captain Walsh. "She lives in Dorchester."

"All the luck," said Flynn.

"Sergeant Whelan has been assigned to you for some time now, Flynn. Repeatedly he has asked to be transferred to some other duty."

"I've encouraged every request, haven't I, Grover? I've made a few requests to that point of my own."

Walsh said, "Every request of his has been denied. Although I've personally endorsed every one of them."

"My requests to have him removed from underfoot have been denied, too. I wonder why that is."

"The reason is, Frank, that you're not a trained police officer. You did not come up through the ranks. You don't know the protocol. You don't even know the vocabulary."

"True," admitted Flynn. "I have no imagination at all."

"You suddenly appeared from nowhere, were given the nonexistent rank of 'Inspector,' and since have been riding roughshod through police and court procedure, frequently leaving nothing short of disaster in your wake. You screw up the paperwork. You not only show no loyalty to your fellow officers, frequently you seem deliberately to make fools of them."

"Impossible."

"Sergeant Whelan has been assigned to you to keep you straight. From what he's told me, he's had a miserable life trying."

Flynn said, "My intentions are good."

"I have the sense, even now, talking to you, that you're laughing at me. Are you?"

"You must be misinterpreting my natural cheery good nature."

"Sergeant Whelan has provided me with a detailed report on you, Flynn." Walsh thumbed the pages of a manuscript the size of a Ph.D. thesis. "Names. Dates. Have I said enough already about your frequent and ridiculously excused absences from work?"

"You have."

"You seem to have a retired police officer working for you full-time without compensation. One Walter Concannon."

Flynn said, "I do not."

At the side of the room, Grover said, "Liar! Cocky is retired on half pay. He has no right even to be involved in police matters, investigations. He has no right even to be in the building! Let alone, tell me what to do."

Flynn smiled at Grover.

"All right." Walsh raised the palm of his hand in the air. "Tell me, Inspector, just where does Lieutenant Walter Concannon, Retired, live?"

"I've never asked him."

"You do not know where he lives?"

"I do not."

"He lives in some hole in the Old Records Building," Grover asserted.

"Is that true?" Walsh tried to fix his watery eyes on Flynn's.

"What's truth?" Flynn asked.

"I don't wonder you ask." Walsh looked back at his papers.

"A good one," Flynn said.

"Sergeant Whelan reports you live in a three-story Victorian house in Winthrop overlooking Boston Harbor."

"And just under all the main flight patterns into and out of Logan International Airport. Terrible roarings and crashings and boomings go on all day and all night. It's a wonder my ears are still as astute as they are."

"We can find no record that your home is mortgaged to a local bank."

Flynn said nothing.

"That's unusual, for a police officer, don't you think? You have five children. Four of them attend private school. Their annual tuition, combined, about consumes your annual income from the Boston Police Department."

"I run an old car."

"That's another thing," Grover expostulated. "He uses me like a personal chauffeur. An errand boy! In city-owned vehicles! He makes me pick him up at his house in the morning, bring him home at night, take his kids to that damned snotty Cartwright School they go to . . ."

"Is it true you own a farm in Ireland, Flynn?"

"The kids have told me so," Grover asserted. "It's called Locked Phooey or something. Typical!"

"How do you afford all this, Flynn?"

"Don't forget his girlfriend," Grover urged. "Mrs. Fleming. The Judge's widow."

"Girlfriend!" Flynn said to Walsh. "I believe you know Dr. Sarah Fleming. A professor of criminology who consults with this department?"

Grover said, "She rides a pink motorcycle."

Walsh hitched his desk chair. Again he thumbed Grover's thesis. "Then there's a complete record of your not exactly bringing people to justice. What is it the newspapers call you? 'Reluctant' Flynn? Cases where Dicky tells me you have more than enough evidence to charge a suspect with crime, bring the case to court, and, for some reason, you don't? He's documented many such cases."

"Sassie Fleming, for one," Grover said. "She murdered her husband! She murdered over a hundred people! She's rich! She was never charged!"

"Is that so, Flynn?"

"He never let me charge his damned sons for knocking me down on a Cambridge street, either!"

"Grover," Flynn said patiently. "Cambridge is outside our jurisdiction. Another city altogether. You've taught me that."

"What was all that about, Flynn?"

"Grover misunderstood instructions," Flynn said. "Sometimes the lad's enthusiasm causes him to forget the object of our exercise."

"My name's not Grover!" shouted Sergeant Richard T. Whelan. Now his face was very flushed. "It's Dick!"

"Ah, what's wrong with my having a pet name for you, Grover? Somehow I can't bring myself to call you a Dick."

"What is a Grover?" Walsh asked.

"A creature which travels close to the ground, I think," Flynn said. "Seldom looks either up or to all sides of himself. Myopic, whose little legs travel him faster than he can apprehend either directions or dangers."

"That's another thing," Grover said. "He's always sayin' things no one understands. We're sick of it!"

"Is a grover some kind of a mythical character, Frank?"

"I wish."

Walsh squared himself to his desk. "I went to Boston Latin School."

"I'm sure the old place is proud of you."

"Well, Frank. I'm going to give you a choice. Resign."

"But, Captain, you don't understand. I am resigned."

"Is that another one of your jokes?"

"Not really."

"Or, while you are suspended from duty, Internal Affairs will do a thorough investigation of all affairs concerning 'Inspector' Francis Xavier Flynn. Such an investigation will probably take months. The way you spend money, you'll probably have to get another job, or jobs, anyway. The first thing IA will require from you are your income tax filings and financial statements for the last seven years. Have you been in this country seven years?"

"Yes and no."

"Having feelings for you as a fellow police officer, of however short a duration, feelings you do not have for others, I strongly suggest you resign. If you wish to avoid an investigation, the commissioner should have your resignation on his desk tomorrow morning."

Grover looked as if he'd heard Santa's sleigh land on the roof.

Walsh asked Flynn, "What do you think of me now, Frank Flynn?"

Flynn said, "I see you've never been in Afghanistan."

The intercom on Walsh's desk buzzed. He pushed the button. "Yes?"

"Captain, the commissioner called to ask Inspector Flynn to come to his office right away. He heard Inspector Flynn is in the building."

Grover beamed. "I sent a copy of my report to him, too."

Captain Walsh said into his intercom, "Tell the commissioner we'll all be there right away."

———

"What's this?" Police Commissioner Edward D'Esopo looked up from his desk as Inspector Francis Xavier Flynn, Captain Timothy Walsh, and Sergeant Richard T. Whelan paraded into his office. "Who sent for you guys?"

"You did," said Captain Walsh.

"I did?" D'Esopo looked at his assistant, Captain Reagan, sitting in a side chair. Reagan was dressed, as always, in full parade uniform, down to brass buttons and gold braid. "What do you guys want?"

Captain Walsh sat in a chair facing the commissioner. Grover lingered behind him.

Flynn wandered over to the floor-to-ceiling windows fourteen stories over the city.

"I've had a good discussion with Inspector Flynn," Walsh said. "Explained his options to him: either resign or face a long and thorough investigation by Internal Affairs."

"You have?"

"I have. After studying the report prepared by Sergeant Richard T. Whelan, which doubtlessly you haven't had time to study fully."

"I have studied it. Fully." D'Esopo looked at Grover. "Are you Sergeant Richard T. Whelan?"

Grover nodded enthusiastically.

"Flynn's problems can be boiled down simply." Walsh adopted the kindly manner of speech of one of his teachers at Boston Latin School, long since dead. "First, there are Inspector Flynn's frequent, prolonged absences from work, for which he offers the most ridiculous excuses: supposedly he's had his appendix removed twice; he's buried his mother five times . . ."

D'Esopo frowned at Reagan.

"Then there's the matter of his questionable finances. Owns a large, mortgage-free house on the water in Winthrop; he owns a farm in Ireland—"

"Locked Phooey," Grover said.

"—has four children in private school—"

"Went to the wrong courtroom this morning." Grover grinned in Flynn's direction. "He was supposed to go to Courtroom 6 but went to Courtroom 9 instead."

"Did he?" Walsh asked with great interest.

"Who is this guy?" D'Esopo asked Reagan. "Sergeant Richard T. Wailing? Whatever?"

"Captain Timothy Walsh's nephew," Reagan said. "Promoted ahead of his time, you might say. Ahead of your time, too. We put him over in the Old Records Building with Frank to keep him out of harm's way."

Flynn muttered, "He's Grover."

D'Esopo asked the standing sergeant: "You're Grover?"

Grover nodded less enthusiastically.

"Well, we can fix that." To Reagan: "Are we still planning nightly foot patrols in the combat zone?"

Reagan said, "Eddy, you might as well send Grover directly to the emergency room at Boston City Hospital."

D'Esopo cleared his throat. "Are you applying for early retirement, Timothy?"

"Me?" Captain Walsh's nose reddened. "No. At my age? Whatever made you think that?"

"It seems to me that you are."

"How can you say that?"

"It seems to me you're questioning my judgment."

"That's a very good way to win early retirement, Timothy," Reagan advised him.

"Why are you questioning Inspector Flynn at all, Timothy?"

"Grave irregularities concerning Flynn have come to my attention, Eddy. Commissioner. I outrank 'Inspector' Flynn. So—"

"Who says you do?"

"I'm a captain, Eddy. I have the duty—"

"We only have one inspector, Timothy. I assigned Francis Xavier Flynn the rank of inspector. How do you know I didn't mean the rank of 'inspector,' as you belch the word, higher than the rank of 'captain'?"

"Is it?"

"It is, if I say it is. Captain Walsh, do you know everything about everything?"

"Well, no. I'd never say—"

"Then what makes you think you know where Francis Xavier Flynn came from, why he's here, what he's doing here . . . even who he is?"

"Well, I guess I don't. If you put it that way."

"Do you think I run such a sloppy police department I don't well know Frank has had his appendix out twice? I visited him, personally, in the hospital, both times. That his mother has died five times? I attended every funeral, myself. Even sent flowers. I've heard this morning Inspector Flynn's mother is feeling poorly again, poor dear."

"Eddy, I didn't mean—"

"To stick your nose in where it doesn't belong? I suggest you take your nephew, Sergeant Richard T. Whining, downstairs, and each stick your nose in a cup of strong, black coffee."

Captain Walsh jumped up, to obey.

"And after you've done that, Sergeant Richard T. Writhing, go get a car, and wait for Inspector Flynn outside the front door. I suspect shortly he'll want to go to Cambridge."

Grover said, "Cambridge isn't in our jurisdiction."

D'Esopo looked at Reagan.

Reagan said, "Go along, there's a good lad, Grover. Do as we tell you. Take Inspector Flynn to Cambridge, then to his home; then go to your own wee nest, make a nice fire of your written report on Inspector Flynn, and try not to burn your fingers any more than you already have."

Before leaving his office, Sergeant Richard T. Whelan turned and said to Captain Reagan: "My name's not Grover."

His was the face of the four-year-old who had confused Christmas with April Fools' Day.

FIVE

"Frank," Commissioner Eddy D'Esopo asked. "How do you know the President of Harvard University?"

"I don't think I do," Flynn said. "Of course, one meets all sorts on a bus."

"He seems to know you."

"Does he?"

"He called me personally asking if I would ask you to make some time for him today. At your convenience."

"I've heard Harvards have nice manners. Shall we have him up for tea?"

"He asked if you are out of town."

"Am I?"

"He said he called your home yesterday. Left a message asking you to return his call."

"That he did," Flynn said. "Come to think of it."

Captain Reagan chuckled. "If the President of Harvard University called me, I think I'd remember it. A lifetime. I think I'd return his call, too."

"I was half asleep when Elsbeth told me. I'd just returned

from doing a bit of surgery in a graveyard, you know, tree surgery, depending on your perspective—"

D'Esopo looked at Reagan. "What's he talking about?"

"Who knows?" Reagan shrugged. "Who ever knows?"

"Have you ever been in the mansion of the President of Harvard University, Frank?"

"Not that I remember."

Reagan chuckled.

"God." The commissioner sighed. "I'd love to see inside that place. Anyway, now's your chance. Captain Reagan will call and say you're on your way."

"Any idea what this is about?" Flynn asked. "Lost dog? Cat up a tree? Noisy neighbors, do you suppose?"

"Probably wants your advice, Frank, on how to invest their multibillion-dollar endowment."

"Ah, could that be it? I'll offer them my idea regarding billboards. I'm sure there's a profit to be made there."

"Billboards?" Reagan awaited the punch line.

"Yes," Flynn drawled. "Some billboards should be blurry."

"Blurry billboards?"

"Yes. For those who leave their eyeglasses at home."

Reagan and D'Esopo enjoyed their laugh.

"Sure." Flynn looked around the big, bright office. "Isn't the world a better place without Grover and Timothy Walsh?"

"God." D'Esopo fiddled with a pen on his desk. "That came off the wall at us. I admit it is hard for us, Frank, to cover the fact that you have obligations to another agency." He raised and lowered his shoulders. "Whatever agency. I suggest that we try to do a better job at making excuses for you. Who would have thought anyone would be watching our paperwork so closely? We've been a little playful with it."

"You can afford to lose a kidney, Frank." Reagan smiled broadly. "You have two of those."

"Kidney next time," Flynn agreed. "Then perhaps I'll be ready for a brain transplant."

"The brain of a pig, Frank?" Reagan was enjoying himself. "I understand pigs are smarter than they look."

"No one would notice the difference, I'm sure. But, while I have at least half my wits about me, hasn't the time come now for me to be relieved of Grover? No human scares me more than the stupid person who thinks he's clever."

"Can't, Frank." D'Esopo was firm on the topic. "We can't justify assigning anyone to you who may have a real future with the department."

"Anyone who is capable of doing good work," seconded Reagan. "Just use Grover as your go-for, your gopher?" Reagan's eyes lit up. "That's what you've really been calling him all these years! I'll be damned! That's the first thing I've ever understood about you, Flynn! Am I right?"

D'Esopo said, "Keep the idiot squelched."

Flynn prepared to leave. "Lieutenant Concannon was very happy when I saw him this afternoon. I do believe he would have been jumpin' up and down with glee, if he were able."

"Good." D'Esopo looked at Reagan. "You took care of the Cocky matter?"

"I did. He's now on full pay. The income he's lost since

we forced him into early retirement has been made up to him, with interest."

"I trust," Flynn beamed at D'Esopo, "that now Cocky is on full pay, no idiot, say, in Personnel, will think to reassign him, for example, to your staff? He wouldn't be happy elsewhere."

"There is no such idiot," D'Esopo assured Flynn. "I've seen you two work together. You should know by now, Frank, I'm smart enough to let well enough alone."

"That you are, Eddy. That you are. I appreciate that."

"By the way, Flynn," Reagan said. "Remember that the president of the United States can be called Bob or Bill, but the tradition is that the President of Harvard is called The President."

"Is he indeed? I can understand that. My grandmother had a canary once she called The Bird."

The houseman in the white coat repeated, "Inspector Flynn? Boston Police?" Then he said, "Would you wait here a moment, please, sir?"

He went into a room off the foyer from which uttered low murmurs.

"They're saying their prayers in there, from the sounds of it," Flynn said to himself. "Hope they're facing east."

Grover had driven Flynn to Cambridge in stony silence.

While they were going across Massachusetts Bridge, Cocky had called.

"Jackpot, Flynn."

"What is?"

"You've hit the jackpot. You may have found the perfect family, at least as far as crime is concerned."

"And what family is so perfectly criminal?"

"Perfectly non-criminal. The Caprianos."

"Is that so?"

"The original Capriano, Anthony, came here from Italy in 1908. He worked in a butcher shop in Boston five years before starting his own butcher shop in Winthrop, which the family has run ever since. Present owners are Anthony the Third and William. There is a third brother, Francis, who left home at age eighteen and never returned. He is believed to be living in Texas."

"If the third brother is a butcher as well, we can say they're all cutups."

"According to our records, no Capriano has ever been arrested for anything, ever."

"Is that so unusual?"

"Not even for speeding. Not even for illegal parking."

"Maybe they haven't cars."

"They have cars. Children. Dogs. Property."

"Do you know anything else about them?"

"Therefore, not much. They are all members of the local Roman Catholic church, St. Jude's. The brothers work six full days a week in their store. Together they own a summer house on a lake in Maine, which one brother's family uses in July, the other in August. No complaints against them in the State of Maine, either. Ever."

"Saintly people, it appears. Thank you, Lieutenant."

Trailed by the houseman, Judge Goldston entered the foyer of Harvard's presidential mansion.

"Flynn?"

"Judge Goldston."

"You went to Harvard?"

"Just to the libraries."

"I'm surprised to see you here. A little off your beat, aren't you?"

"The President asked to see me."

"I see. Gerald, I think you should take Inspector Flynn up to the President's private study right away. I'll tell him you're here, Frank."

"Thank you."

Flynn followed the houseman up two flights of stairs to a small room at the back of the house. Leaving, the houseman did not close the door.

The room overlooked parts of Harvard Yard, Lamont Library, Houghton Library. The room was book-lined. There was a faded crimson rug on the floor. There were a few photographs on the handsome wooden desk facing a window.

Closing the door behind him, the President said, "Thank you for coming, Mr. Flynn." They shook hands.

"A comfortable room," Flynn said.

"This is where I choose to be, when I have a choice. I seldom bring anyone else here. Would you like a drink?"

"I had a drink, once. I didn't much like it."

"I see. Have you a room like this, somewhere?"

"I have a nice office. Quiet."

"I would like to visit you in your private office, someday."

"You'd be most welcome. Do you play chess?"

"I play no games."

"I think I understand that."

"I understand you're musical." The President indicated a small stereo in a bookcase within reach of his desk chair. "Are you able to have a stereo of some sort in your office?"

"I listen to recorded music as seldom as possible."

"Why is that?"

"Today's recordings are too good. Too enhanced? I believe they spoil the ears for live music."

"Yes. Interesting." He pointed out a photograph on his desk. "Do you know who that is?"

"Professor Louis Loveson."

"Yes. Ever read him?"

"His volume *The Ontologic,* yes. Also his *Usable Past.* Some time ago."

"It's about him I wish to speak. Do sit down. I've been unsure as to what to do, how to do it. Finally I brought the matter up to John Roy Priddy."

"I thought I'd hear his name this afternoon."

"No Name has been very good to Harvard, especially to the Kennedy Government Center. We've had much advice from John Roy regarding matters 'between the borders.' You spoke at the Kennedy Center a few years ago yourself. 'An Understanding of Islamic Fundamentalism.'"

"Were you there?"

"I heard people talking about it. So I read the transcript."

"There was a transcript?"

"Harvard has heavy archival responsibilities, Mr. Flynn. By the way, I thought you were dead."

"I try to be."

"Not dead, just sleeping, is that it?"

"Trying not to be the object of the attention of K. and other such people. Even if they do know me to be alive, they believe me less of a threat to them these days."

"N. N. 13. You must have been very successful to attain such high rank."

"What about Professor Loveson?"

"He's not only a great teacher—he was my beloved teacher when I was here as a student—but he is my great friend."

"You're lucky."

"Yes. But something is wrong. In recent years he's gone from one of our most beloved teachers to one of our most reviled. He is held in contempt, initially by most of his colleagues, now by an ever-increasing percentage of the student body. Ten years ago, it was difficult for students to get into any of his two courses. Now he has only one course, with only seven people in it."

"Why?"

"I don't think it's caused by anything he's done or said. Is that what I mean? I mean, I don't believe he's changed. I don't know why."

"He must be rather along in years."

"Seventy-six. By understandings, of course, he should have retired. When he found himself increasingly reviled, he stated his desire to continue teaching, until there was some satisfactory conclusion."

"What is it people are saying about him?"

"That he's dishonest? Can you believe that?"

"I'm not sure what they mean."

"Neither am I."

"I don't see how I can help."

"A woman who was his teaching assistant about seven years ago has come to me . . . She says she thinks Louie is being assaulted."

"Assaulted? Who would assault a seventy-six-year-old professor?"

"Threatened. She believes he's been receiving phone calls, notes. She said she saw such a note on his desk at the library. He snapped it away from her immediately."

"Physically threatening him? With bodily harm?"

"I believe so. I've asked him about it. He denies it."

"Some person or persons are threatening to kill him?"

"I don't know. He needs a friend, Flynn. Someone to stand with him, find out all about this, someone who will know what to do if push comes to shove, if you know what I mean. I'm President of this university. Obviously I can't do, well, more than I've tried."

"If you're asking about police protection . . ."

"No. He utterly rejected the thought of that. He wants his privacy. His wife isn't well. If it's any help to your matters of protocol, his apartment is in Boston. Isn't that within your jurisdiction?"

"If he won't talk . . ."

"You know, I rather think in some odd way he's rather ashamed of this situation. At least, in front of his colleagues. In front of me. You're not a member of the university, or the teaching profession. You're a policeman. Yet you aren't. If you're willing to be helpful here, I will try to explain you to him, best I can. It will help that you actually read his books."

"I'm not sure how helpful I can be."

"Are you willing to try?"

"Well, yes. But the actual time I can spend with him will be necessarily limited. I have other duties, court appearances . . ."

"I understand. It's more a matter of your getting to the bottom of whatever is going on, and making it stop, if possible. If my perception that he is ashamed of this situation is correct . . . I'll assure him you will not be reporting to me, or to the police commissioner, or to anyone. Will that be all right? Are you allowed to spend time on something of this sort without having to file reports?"

"Oh, yes."

The President took papers out of a drawer of the table beside him. "Here is a copy of his biography from *Who's Who in America*. This other paper just has his address, phone number, where his office is, where and when he teaches his little class—that sort of thing."

"Thank you."

"I suppose it would be correct for Harvard to offer to pay your expenses . . ."

"No. Professor Loveson is a citizen, a taxpayer. He deserves our protection, to whatever extent—"

"That's good. I really don't want a written record of this, if you understand me. Unless, of course, something happens and it is unavoidable."

"Let's hope nothing happens."

"Exactly."

"Do you know where the Professor is now?"

"He's in his office. But at six o'clock he's due at a departmental cocktail party at his dean's house. The address is on that paper. I've urged him not to attend such functions, but he insists. He now attends more such things than he ever has in his life. He's a stubborn old man, Mr. Flynn."

"Good for him."

"Good as long as he's safe," the President said. "I, personally, don't want an incident. Obviously, the university does not want an incident. I would like Professor Loveson to have the peace and respect he deserves in his later years. Don't you agree?"

"Whatever that means. In this case."

SIX

Inside the front door of Dean Wincomb's small Victorian home on a Cambridge side street was a stuffed umbrella stand. Bicycles were on each side of the hall.

After puzzling the dean's wife by introducing himself, explaining his presence only by saying he was there to meet Professor Louis Loveson, Flynn stepped into the living room. He stood to one side.

And was ignored.

Again he had left the silently obedient Grover in the car.

Flynn considered the subtle changes in the academics in the room from those he had known of a previous generation. For the most part, they were physically more trim. A few looked as if they spent more time jogging and lifting weights than in the library stacks.

There were more women, of course.

The room also seemed curiously partitioned. In the center of the room, five women talked together. A group of four comprised only Asians. Three blacks, two men and a woman, stood separately. One man and the woman affected something resembling African garb. Groups of white males were segregated by age, from roughly twenty-five to forty and from forty to sixty-five.

And these groups seemed to be ignoring each other.

Even the dean did not appear to be circulating among his guests.

Were the eyes of all these people more intense because their ideas were more intense, or because they spent so much time concentrating on computer screens?

Did they all speak more loudly because of their strong convictions, or because their hearing had been impaired by years of overamplified music as students?

Or did they speak more loudly competitively?

The few who looked his way did not seem to see him, really. If they were seeing him, they were dismissing him not as an unknown but as an irrelevancy.

Flynn was entertaining himself with these observations when Professor Louis Loveson entered the room. Flynn remained standing aside, watching silently.

The professor was a great deal thinner than the photo of him Flynn had just seen on the President's desk. The joyful twinkle of wisdom in the professor's eyes had been replaced by sadness.

The sound level lowered when the professor entered the room. People only glanced at him. They did not smile. No one greeted him.

It seemed to Flynn as if no one in the room wanted to be overheard by Professor Loveson.

As the professor moved slowly to the bar table and made himself a whiskey and ginger ale, people, even with their backs to him, moved just a step or two away from him.

The professor then moved away from the bar table. He turned his face toward the room. Clearly he was willing to be engaged in conversation.

Still no one approached him.

Flynn watched only a moment longer.

"Professor Loveson . . ."

"I was told someone would speak to me this evening, by the name of Flynn." The professor sipped his drink. "Are you that Flynn?"

"I am."

"You are here to befriend me."

"Something of the sort."

Loveson appeared to be measuring the relative smallness of Flynn's head versus the hugeness of his shoulders and chest. "Stand with me, as it were, against the vestiges of what appears to be my fate?"

Flynn said, "Simply, you have a friend who cares a great deal about you. He would like to be here, standing with you, but he cannot be. He doesn't understand what is happening to you. Around you."

"Whoever really understands what is happening to him, while it is happening? Our best choice is to remain open, available, observant, and surmise what we can as we go along. Don't you agree?"

"You also have the choice to turn your back to those who turn their backs to you . . ."

"Have I? Some of the people in this room were my students, Mr. Flynn. They came from near and far, mostly with all the strange bricks, family, church, community, a certain education, if I may make a pun, arrogance, materialism, prejudice, racism, sexism, anti-intellectualism, even anti-culturalism in their ill-built foundations. Everyone in this room has studied my works. Including you, I understand."

"Yes."

"I want to know what it is I have done to them—or not done for them. Surely you can understand that?"

"After spending ten minutes in this room," Flynn said, "I can say you care more for these people than perhaps they deserve. I have always understood Harvards have manners."

"No, no. I care for myself. My work. How would you feel, Mr. Flynn, if, at the age of seventy-six, you could not draw up a list of people willing to be your pallbearers?"

"Good God, man. What a way to think."

"Yes," Loveson looked at the floor. "What a thing to think. How have I dug my own grave? Now must I crawl to it, and fall into it unattended?"

Flynn looked at all the backs in the room. "Have you accomplished what you came here to accomplish?"

"Oh, yes." Loveson put his half-empty glass neatly on a coaster. "We'll go now. But first I must thank our hostess for having me. Some of us Harvards still pretend to manners. Just habit, really."

"Is this a police car?" Professor Loveson looked around the backseat and at equipment strange to him in the front of the car.

Flynn said, "Yes. Driven by Police Sergeant Richard T. Whelan. This is Professor Louis Loveson, Grover. You have his address."

Grover sighed.

"Perhaps we shouldn't talk while the sergeant is driving," Loveson said. "These Cambridge streets are so dangerous."

"Especially when Grover is driving."

"I've never been in a police car before."

"Good for you."

"I've ridden donkeys, elephants, troop carriers, of course, but I've never been in a police car before." He patted the backseat. "Have real criminals sat here on this seat, do you suppose? Murderers, rapists, plagiarists?"

"I suppose so. More forgers, I suspect, than plagiarists."

"Is there a difference?"

"We're better at catching forgers, aren't we, Grover?"

Loveson said, "This rather brings home to me the reality of my situation. How ashamed my father would be to know I had ever ridden in a police car. Under any circumstances."

To Flynn the professor seemed exceedingly small, sitting next to him on the backseat. Flynn's fifteen-year-old sons were bigger. Even Winny, at nine, had more substance, more presence than him. As the car went under streetlights, nothing but bone outlined the knees of the professor's gray trousers.

"Tell me, Professor," Flynn said. "What would you think if you came across a young man, sixteen years old, to be exact, standing tall against a tree in a foggy wood at night, with his ear nailed close to the tree?"

Wide-eyed, Grover turned around and looked at Flynn.

"Have you ever?" Loveson asked.

"Last night."

"Really! How very interesting. You see, that's what I mean. André Gide once wrote, 'When all else is forgotten, what remains is culture.' Core culture, I call it. Of what ethnic is this boy?"

"Italian American."

"Yes. European, surely. And this happened locally?"

"Yes."

"A strange and simple act of that sort, nailing a boy's ear to a tree, quite common in fifteenth-century Europe, for example, suddenly turns up last night in the Boston area. Probably there has been no such incident on these shores, well, ever before."

"Someone could have just made it up, invented it for himself, thought it an amusing thing to do."

"The idea, possibly," Loveson said. "But not the attitude behind the idea."

"And how do you describe that attitude?" Flynn asked. "The attitude that makes nailing a boy's ear to a tree seem a good idea?"

"Punitive, of course. More than that. To mortify him. Wouldn't you say?"

In the front seat, Grover banged the steering wheel with the butt of his hand.

"Did you help the boy get free of the tree, Flynn?"

"Yes."

"Why?"

"I might not have, if I knew who had nailed him to the tree and why."

"He wouldn't tell you?"

"He would not. Once he understood something of the history of his situation, that he had been left there to rip his own ear from the tree, he assured me he would do so immediately after I left. I believed him."

"Saying is quite else from doing."

"Also, my daughter is fond of him. I think she prefers him with two flappy ears, instead of one."

"Ah, daughters! I remember. I had one once. She could get me to do, or not do, anything. Sergeant Whelan, I live in this block. Halfway down on the right." To Flynn, Loveson said, "Your daughter's young friend displeased someone, or some persons, in a very particular way."

"What way?" Flynn asked. "What would be the nature of his crime to cause someone to nail his ear to a tree?"

Loveson said, "I suspect he did something unmanly."

"'Unmanly'!"

"Sorry I can't invite you in, Flynn—"

Flynn had gotten out of the car first. "You are inviting me in, Professor. I need to see where and how you live, for security reasons, if for none other. And to talk with you further."

On the curb, he took Loveson's elbow in hand.

The professor looked up to read Flynn's eyes. Suddenly, he regained the wise twinkle in his own. "It's either that or you'll take me downtown to Headquarters, is that it? Do you still use a rubber hose?"

"Of course," Flynn said. "How else do you make the daisies grow?"

"Well, all right." Loveson began to step across the sidewalk. "Don't blame me for anything you see. Or hear. Or think. Or smell."

———◆———

The apartment did smell.

Flynn didn't know what to think.

It was a small apartment, third-floor front in a building

61

overlooking the Charles River across Storrow Drive. It looked as if it had been furnished all at once about forty years before and unchanged since then.

The heavy woman already dressed in an overcoat and clearly waiting to leave stood up from a chair in the living room and headed for the front door as soon as Professor Loveson and Flynn entered.

"All right, Mrs. McElroy." Loveson held the door open for her. "A little late tonight. Had a meeting to attend. Everything went well?"

Flynn stepped out of her path.

"As well as can be expected."

She smelled of gin.

Loveson closed the door behind her. "Dear Mrs. McElroy," Loveson said. "Don't know what we'd do without her."

In the living room an obese woman with huge eyes sat in a chair under a blanket.

"Hello, old dear." Loveson kissed her on the cheek. "This is my wife, Mr. Flynn. She hasn't been as well as she might be lately; have you, old dear?"

Her huge eyes seemed to be consuming Flynn like something edible.

"I've brought you Mr. Flynn."

"Where do you live, Mr. Flynn?"

"Winthrop."

"Winthrop House?"

"No, my dear. He's not associated with Harvard. Mr. Flynn works with the Boston Police Department. I'll get you your dinner as soon as I have my own."

"That's all right," she said.

The kitchenette was separated from a dining area, a living area by only a counter.

Loveson poured cereal into two bowls. "I don't suppose you want any of this?"

"Is that your supper?"

"I was never strong in the domestic department. I have a good, albeit solitary lunch, at the Faculty Club each day. Mrs. McElroy provides Callie with a good hot dinner at midday."

"I'll bet she does."

"Bathes her. Cleans up."

Flynn looked around the apartment. Nothing was clean. There were stacks of old magazines surrounding Callie Loveson's chair. The kitchen counter was grimy.

Flynn wondered how much per hour Mrs. McElroy was being paid to sip gin and watch the wallpaper.

Loveson poured milk into his cereal bowl. "Forgive me." He sat at a small kitchen table to eat. "Callie expects me to keep to a schedule, at least until I put her to bed."

"Louie?" Callie called from the living area. "Will we be moving to Boston soon?"

"Yes, old dear. Soon."

"But have you arranged for an apartment there for us yet?"

"Yes, old dear. I did that last weekend while I was up having my final interviews at Harvard. A nice, bright apartment. Two bedrooms. It overlooks the Charles River."

"That's nice," she said.

"You'll have to furnish it, of course."

"Have we the money? I mean, to furnish it?"

"Enough. From the advance on my *Ontologic* book."

"Oh, yes," she said. "You told me that."

"Now, Mr. Flynn." Loveson looked at his guest as if he were shifting languages instead of eras. "Where do we start?"

"You are being threatened?"

"No."

"You have not received threatening notes? Phone calls?"

"No."

"You don't seem surprised by my question."

"I forgot to." Loveson smiled. "Act surprised, that is. I should have, shouldn't've I?"

"You're not a practiced liar."

"No. I am not a practiced liar."

"How can we help you, if you are not honest with us?"

"There's nothing you can do. I'm an old man. I suppose I wouldn't be a problem at all, if I didn't care about what happens to the world in this and future generations; if I turned my back on all and sundry, which you mentioned as something I might do. But I do care. Enormously. Just part of my habit, I suppose. Like manners."

"We need to know if you are in physical danger. If so, we need to find out the source of that danger."

"And do what? Change everyone's mind? That's a teacher's job. Not a policeman's."

"Would it mean anything to you if I said the university does not want an incident?"

"The university is having plenty of incidents."

"I mean a violent incident. Concerning you."

"I would welcome it. Knocking me off—is that proper police parlance?—might clarify things considerably."

"Not for you."

Loveson poured a little more milk into his cereal bowl. "In your study of history, Flynn, have you ever known a people to—what's the word the young people use these days?—trash their own culture so rapidly?"

"Do you think that is what is happening?"

"We're dazzled by nonlinear toys, the television-computer thing, to which we are relegating our intellectualism, even our spirituality. To say nothing of our basic knowledge, information. Momentarily, time has become rather a jumble. Our sense of synapse is breaking down utterly. Do you see this?"

Flynn said nothing.

"You just said to yourself, 'Louie Loveson is a reactionary. A Luddite.' Am I correct?"

Still, Flynn said nothing.

"Through any era of transition, there must be navigators, as I call them, people who know where we're going based on an understanding of where we've been, and where we are. I'm not against transition, change; quite the contrary."

"You once wrote, 'From conflict comes growth.'"

"I did, yes. Even violent conflict." Loveson continued to spoon the cereal and milk into his mouth. "I believe the natural habitat for these navigators is the university. Yet it seems the university people are those most dazzled by the electronic toy. So where are the navigators?"

"Louie?" Callie Loveson called from the living area. "Have the tickets for the ship arrived yet?"

"Yes, old dear. They were brought to my desk this noon."

"Are they all right? Did you check them?"

"They seem fine. Exactly as we discussed. Starboard side of C Deck."

"I forget what we decided. Are we stopping at Gibraltar or Tangiers?"

"Gibraltar. Then straight on to Alexandria."

"Oh, that's nice. The weather will be lovely there."

"It always is."

Loveson asked Flynn, "Wouldn't you like to look forward, again, to something you did thirty-six years ago?"

Flynn frowned. "I'm not sure."

"That's the point, isn't it?" Loveson grinned. "Selective memory."

Mentally, Flynn was scanning what he remembered of Loveson's *Usable Past.*

He considered the irony of Loveson's work and life.

The telephone rang.

"A good navigator knows," Loveson said, "that everything on a trip depends upon from where you start. And none of that can be forgotten, however things change. Note, for example: last night you came across a young man with his ear nailed to a tree . . ."

Standing, Loveson answered the wall phone. "Yes?"

He said no more.

His face flushed. He hung up.

Flynn said, "You just received a threatening phone call, didn't you?"

"It must have been a wrong number."

"We can have your phone tapped, you know."

"Without my permission?"

Flynn wasn't sure. "Yes."

Loveson poured milk into the second cereal bowl. "I must now feed the old dear, Mr. Flynn. Proceed to wrestle her to bed. It isn't a pretty sight. If you'll forgive me? We'll talk again, I'm sure."

SEVEN

Flynn carried his dinner plate into the dining room. "Where's Todd?"

His family were almost finished with their dinners.

"You know where," Randy said.

"Do I?"

"I'll be doing the same tomorrow night."

"Oh, yes."

Winny asked, "Did you get fired today, Da?"

"Not even fired up." Flynn poured white vinegar on his boiled cabbage. "Had rather an easy day of it, in fact. I discovered that office politics is a great deal easier than real work. No wonder so many people take to it."

"Tell us about Professor Loveson," Elsbeth said. "Such a brilliant man. I thought he was dead."

"All the brilliant people are dead." Jenny was making a stick figure from four remaining strands of corned beef on her plate. "Is what Ms. Smithson-Rourke says."

"Who is Ms. Smithson-Rourke?"

"Oh, Da. You know. Our Soc. teacher."

"We now have someone teaching your socks?"

Winny said, "How pedestrian."

Jenny glared at her little brother. "Social Sciences."

"I think teachers frequently have the impression intellectual history ceases when they are granted their final degree." Flynn put a small dab of Colman's Hot Mustard on his bite of corned beef. "Remind me to send her some books."

"We have Professor Loveson's books here somewhere," Elsbeth said.

"Louis Loveson is alive, and fighting," Flynn answered his wife. "At least he is standing his ground. If I infer correctly, he is fighting for his work. His ideas. Why his ideas are being attacked, and by whom, is the mystery. His ideas always struck me as rather basic, if not downright obvious."

"Is he being physically attacked?" The possibility was not beyond Elsbeth's ken.

"So far, assaulted verbally. Threatened. We think. He's not cooperating a bit. He seems ashamed to admit he receives threatening phone calls, notes."

"Hindi," Elsbeth said.

"Yes."

"Also a touch of Hebrew. 'It must be my fault people are throwing stones at me.' When will we learn?"

"Human," Flynn said.

Randy asked, "People are throwing stones at an old man because of his ideas?"

"People who don't have ideas always throw stones at people who do. It makes them feel better. More equal. Eat your cabbage," Elsbeth said.

Winny intoned, "'Everybody must get stoned.'"

"Why must I eat my cabbage?" Randy asked dramatically. "I don't like cabbage!"

"So you will grow up big and strong and have ideas that make people throw stones at you," his mother answered with equal drama.

"That's an ambition?" Randy asked.

"Yes," Flynn said. "That's the ambition."

"You don't know you've lived until you've been stoned," Winny said.

"Winny!" Jenny's blue orbs blazed at her brother. "Will you shut up!"

"You shut up, you blue-eyed blond girl!"

"Now, Winny," Flynn heard himself saying. "You must be respectful toward your elders."

"You know what Jenny said when Billy Capriano blew in her ear?"

"Winny . . ." Jenny growled.

"What did Jenny say when Billy Capriano blew in her ear?" Flynn asked.

"She said, 'Thanks for the refill!'"

Flynn laughed.

"Da!" Jenny exclaimed. "That's not funny! Don't you laugh at me!"

"I'm laughing at Winny."

Winny snarled at his sister. "You've been picking on me all day. I did not hide your damned hair drier in the damned laundry hamper! I left your damned hair drier in the damned sink!"

Silence around the dinner table.

Finally, Jenny, with suspicion, accusation, disappointment, said: "Da . . . ?"

Flynn cleared his throat. "I did not hide your hair drier in the laundry hamper, either. I found it in the sink. I did put it on the edge of the laundry hamper. It must have fallen in. By itself."

Through Jenny's big blue eyes Flynn could watch her brain doing a swimmer's racing turn.

Shrewdly, she said, "When Winny slammed the door."

———

"So?" At ten-twenty that night Flynn made the day's last trip to the necessarium, as he thought of it.

Todd, having just come home, was in the upper corridor.

"The public high school is abuzz," Todd reported. "This afternoon, Billy Capriano quit the wrestling team."

"Why? What reason did he give?"

"The kids I talked to said he didn't give a reason. No one really knows what he said to the coach. But the coach got mad. People heard him shouting."

"So the inference can be drawn the coach believed Billy's reason for quitting the team was inadequate."

"Any reason short of Billy's having Saint Vitus' dance and the seven-year itch simultaneously would be inadequate, Da. Billy really is a very good wrestler. Even at his age, Billy was expected to make it to the state championship matches in his weight class. I mean we're talking regional, maybe national championship when he's a senior. Major college scholarships."

"That good, is he?"

"He walked home alone."

"What did he do there?"

"I don't know. His father came home a little before five-thirty. Dinner."

"Did angry noises emanate from the house?"

"No. At six-forty, Billy left the house, alone."

"Ha! Now we're gettin' into the good stuff!"

"He walked to St. Jude's Church. They have catechism classes Monday nights."

"Oh."

"He left the church at eight-thirty. Walked home alone."

"Straight home?"

"Yes."

"He spoke to no one on the street? Stopped in nowhere?"

Todd shrugged. "The kid's a straight arrow, Da."

"Have you had something to eat?"

"I made myself a corned-beef sandwich. Milk."

"With plenty of Colman's Hot Mustard?"

"I don't have your leather mouth."

"Got your homework done?"

"I did it in the bushes beside Billy's house. Don't blame me if some teacher calls about my handwriting. The ground is cold."

"Good lad."

"Following people is boring."

Flynn said: "Then be a leader."

Back in bed, Flynn turned out his reading light.

He cuddled Elsbeth.

"Nice kids," he said. "Think it's time we got married?"

"Again? We came from such different backgrounds, places, you and I, over eighteen months we had to get married in three different countries!"

"That's right," Flynn said. "We've each been married three times. I forgot. We're much more fashionable than I thought."

"Three times married to each other. Without benefit of divorce!"

"Golly. Grover might charge me with bigamy."

"May your paperwork never catch up with you, Frannie."

"Not to worry," Flynn said. "I died three times, too. And I can prove it!"

"Next time," Elsbeth said, "leave me insurance."

After Elsbeth fell into the deep breathing of sleep, Flynn asked himself, "Now, why on earth would the Capriano kid quit the wrestling team?"

His dreams that night touched upon some of the rigorous physical exercises he had been put through as a schoolboy in Germany. He had enjoyed that. He didn't even remember ever being too cold in the snow.

EIGHT

"God!" Grover pressed the palms of his hands against each side of his head. "Flynn! What are you doing to me?"

After Professor Loveson's lecture, Grover had preceded Flynn out of the lecture hall, rushed down the stairs, and onto the porch overlooking Harvard Yard.

"In pain are you?" Flynn studied Grover's face in the gray morning light. His skin was grayer than the day. His eyes bulged slightly. During the lecture, Flynn had observed that Grover breathed in increasingly short strokes. "Do you think I'm torturing you? Well, I am. For your sins."

"Torturing me?" Grover looked up the steps at Flynn. Students whirled around them between classes. "That was wonderful!"

"What was?"

"That old man. Professor Lovely?"

"Loveson."

"Well, Loveson's a lovely old man."

"Is he?"

"I've never heard anyone talk that way in my whole life!"

"I daresay."

Driving Flynn from Winthrop to Harvard Square, Grover had protested all the way. His main point was that it was bad enough to use a sergeant of police and a City of Boston vehicle to commute Flynn, "So your wife can use the station wagon," but downright illegal to be using a Boston police vehicle in the City of Cambridge. What were they doing in Cambridge anyway? And at Harvard yet?

As a sergeant of Boston police, Grover stressed to Flynn that he had much better things to do than to ride around outside his own jurisdiction. For one, he was on a committee to prepare for the Policepersons' Ball.

Flynn cursed his impeccable hearing.

Nevertheless, he invited Grover to attend Professor Loveson's lecture with him. It was a raw day.

"I don't know all the words he used, everything he was talking about," Grover admitted, "or the names he used, people he referred to, but I was able to follow along pretty well. He talked for an hour straight!"

"Fifty minutes."

"And he began at the beginning with an idea I didn't much understand, and then he told me more and more about that idea, the history of it, where it came from, what everybody has had to say about it, back and forth, and by the time he finished I felt like I really understood what he had said in the first place! It was like listening to a piece of music! You know, it all hung together."

Flynn stared at his assistant. "And what is the idea that so excites you?"

"Well, first . . ." Grover scraped his shoe on the bottom

step. "That an idea comes from someplace. That it has a history. That it keeps turning up, like, when it's needed. Except every time it turns up, it's fuller somehow. There's more to it."

"What idea in particular?"

Grover said, "I never knew spaghetti originally came from China."

"I see."

Grover's eyes were downcast. Was he embarrassed? "I never knew there's always been an idea of God."

Flynn could think of nothing to say.

Grover's eyes flashed up at Flynn. "It's the idea that's important?"

"And the attitude behind the idea," Flynn ventured. "The need for the idea."

"God." Grover looked at the other students coming and going. "It's the idea that's important?"

"That's the . . ." Flynn could not bring himself to say it.

"Is that what all the kids here are studying?"

Flynn said, "I'm not sure."

"I thought they were just studying to be doctors and lawyers and such like."

"That comes later," Flynn said. "Traditionally, first they're taught to think."

"What a gentleman," Grover marveled. "So gentle. You can tell the way he speaks. Softly, but he makes you listen. He has such respect for all those people he mentioned! He didn't put anyone down! Though I think he likes some better than others."

"Objectivity, it's called."

"Flynn, what are we doing here?"

"With Professor Loveson?"

"Yeah."

"A person or persons unknown may be threatening Professor Loveson."

"Threatening his life?"

"I'm not sure. Assaulting his well-being, his peace of mind, anyway."

Grover's jaw tightened. His eyes flashed. "That fine old gentleman?"

"That 'fine old gentleman' is not cooperating with us at all, at all."

"Is it true you found a kid with his head nailed to a tree?"

"Yes. His ear nailed to a tree."

"What's that got to do with the professor?"

"Nothing. I just wanted to know what he thought about it. I wanted to open him up a bit, to us."

"It wasn't one of your kids, was it?"

"You'd love that, wouldn't you?"

Was this the first time Flynn ever saw Grover smile? "I wouldn't mind."

"Sergeant, I have a full schedule of appointments here today, beginning with lunch with the dean. Why don't you go do whatever, to prepare for the Policepersons' Ball? I'll find my own way back to the office."

"Lucky bastards." Grover glared at the young people milling around in front of the building. "Do they get to feel this buzz in the head all the time? It's a pleasure!" He turned his glare on Flynn. "If anyone, anyone at all, touches one hair on that great man's head, I'll tie him naked in a sack of tomcats and throw him in the Charles River!"

Flynn finally said, "That's the idea."

———

"Isn't education a foine thing?" In the Harvard Faculty Club dining room Flynn pronounced his brogue. "Sure, everyone should be exposed to it at least once."

Across the table from him, Dean Wincomb put boredom rather than humor in his eyes. "Are you a university man yourself, Flynn?"

"I can only claim to a short seminary training."

"Why did you leave?"

"I suspected certainty stunts growth."

The dean's eyes changed to appreciation.

Then the dean said, "Would you like to try the horse meat?"

"I pray I've eaten my last horse. And dog. And snake. And broccoli." Viciously, he rolled the *R*.

The dean ordered lamb chops; Flynn, a venison stew.

"The President's office asked me to lunch with you today. I have no idea why. Of course we did meet last night, at my house."

"We did not meet," Flynn said. "I met no one at your house last night but Professor Louis Loveson. I had to introduce myself to him."

"Yes. Well . . . Therefore I'm guessing you wish to talk to me about Professor Louis Loveson."

The venison stew was brought well before the lamb chops. "Dean, is there reason here for anyone, or any group of people, to be threatening Professor Loveson?"

"'Threatening' him! Good God, no. You don't mean to tell me . . . Actually threatening him?"

"We're not sure."

"Is that why we're having lunch? The President thinks someone might actually be threatening Louis Loveson? Really threatening him? Why would anyone do that?"

"Money is a motive for many crimes. So is position. Prestige. Career advancement."

"Not in a university, Flynn! I think you can trust us to be a little more . . ."

"A little more what?"

"Trust us to keep a schooled perspective on such things as greed, ambition."

Flynn tilted his head. "You say that with a straight face?"

The chops were served.

The stew had cooled.

"I was engaged in no conversation at your house last evening, Dean, except, briefly, with Professor Loveson. Would you list for me the topics of conversation you had with those with whom you did speak?"

"Well . . . Well . . ." A blue tinge came into the dean's face. "Well, no! I won't."

"Did you speak on intellectual matters?"

"Of course."

"Of students?"

"Surely."

"Of new writings?"

"We must have."

"Remarkable," Flynn said. "Every such meeting I've ever attended has been devoted to career politics. Your little get-together last evening must have been a first."

"I really don't know what this is about, Mr. Flynn—"

"Nor do I. Trying to get my footing, as it were. What, simply, do people have against Professor Louis Loveson?"

"For starters, he's rather the President's pet."

"And that causes resentment?"

"You might say so. If he weren't, for example, I might be having lunch at my desk playing a computer game rather than sitting here listening to your grave suspicions regarding university politics. Are you familiar with the game, 'What if . . . ?,' Flynn? You know, What if John Kennedy hadn't been shot? What if—?"

"No, sir. I have come to assume that is the province of contemporary journalism."

The dean frowned. "Loveson's a good topic for the 'What if . . . ?' game. What if he had retired when he was supposed to?"

"What if, indeed?" asked Flynn.

"For one thing, his academic chair, the prestigious Samson Chair, would have been vacated."

"And awarded to whom?"

"There are several sterling candidates."

"Would your name be among them?"

"No. I haven't the reputation."

"Loveson did not retire as expected," stated Flynn. "Last night he indicated to me that was because he feels he must defend himself, his work, by staying on."

"Some consider his work indefensible."

"Do you?"

"Oh, it enjoyed its fashion. One might see it as the intellectual swan song of the white male. You know, Western culture tied into a neat package."

Flynn nodded. "Again, talking with him last night, I had the impression he cares a great deal for his students. Past, present, and future."

"I suspect the old boy feels he must defend them against the barbarians at the gates."

"And who are these barbarians?"

"Anyone who isn't a white male in the Judeo-Christian tradition. All rather medieval, of course. Anyway, he has damned few students at present. Seven, I think is the number. We have him in the smallest lecture hall available. We'd put him in a telephone booth, if we could still find one with a door on it."

"And why does he attract so few students now?"

"He still believes in the superiority of one idea over another, you see."

"Ah! One of those, is he?"

The dean gave Flynn a sharp look. "He's still teaching intellectual history, Flynn, the history of ideas as a continuum. As if it were all a straight line. A logical progression."

"And history cannot be seen that way?"

"Well, it can, of course. Rather egocentric, don't you think?"

"'Egocentric.'" Flynn mulled the word.

"Egocentric." The dean was enjoying his bite of lamb chop. "Wouldn't you consider it a luxury to be able to select the ideas which permit you to justify whatever you are thinking at the moment?"

"Now, wasn't I taught there's a difference between being rational and rationalizing?"

Finished with his two bites of his two lamb chops, the

dean seemed exasperated by his peas. "Are you still dealing with such a concept, Flynn? 'The rational'?"

"I prefer an idea that works to one which doesn't work as well. Isn't that rational?"

"'Doesn't work as well' in whose judgment?"

"Mine."

"There you are." The dean smiled. "The egocentric white male."

"More an everyman." Flynn pretended to shiver. "Terrified of chaos."

"But what may be chaotic to your view, may not be chaotic to another person's view."

The dean gave up on his peas. "Didn't you just say something about 'certainty stunting growth'?"

"I did. Yes. You have me there."

The dean sipped his iced tea. "What are you, Mr. Flynn? Some sort of policeman?"

"Some sort."

"And how much rationality do you see on the streets in your function as a policeman?"

"Yes." Flynn nodded his head. "Chaos terrifies me."

———————

"Mr. Flynn?"

A woman in a tailored suit carrying a canvas bag of books rose from a chair in the foyer of the Faculty Club.

"Yes?"

"I believe I'm on your schedule to be interviewed. Or is 'questioned' the right word? I'm Francine Huong."

"Dr. Huong, is it?"

"Yes. Some years ago I was Dr. Loveson's teaching assistant. I saw you lunching with Dean Wincomb. You're probably in a hurry."

"Not at all. You weren't at the soiree at the dean's home last night, Dr. Huong."

"No. I never attend such ice-cube fights." She looked around the foyer. She nodded at two chairs. "If you have the time, we could talk there?"

"Certainly."

Sitting, she said, "I'm very, very fond of Louie Loveson. His life is being threatened."

"The President told me you say so."

"About three weeks ago, I was in his office looking for a magazine he said he would leave for me. A book was open on his desk. What he seemed to be using as a bookmark was odd-shaped and colorful. I thought perhaps some child had made it for him. It was only natural for me to look at it." Her chin and her voice lowered. "It read, 'U die within month.' The word 'You' was just written with a capital *U*, do you understand?"

"That's very odd."

"Why?"

"Not very academic, is it?"

"I suppose not. But anybody—"

"Yes. Anybody."

"Louie came in. When he saw what I was looking at, he snapped it from my hand. Mr. Flynn, I've known and worked with Louie Loveson for years. Never have I seen him angry. About anything. When he grabbed that piece of paper from me, there was horrible anger in his eyes. At me!"

"That's odd, too. Anger at your seeing it, instead of at the note itself?"

"Yes. I tried to ask him about it. I was stammering. In shock, at seeing what the note said. At seeing his anger. He yelled at me. He waved his arm at me. 'Get out! Get out!'"

"Three weeks ago, you said."

"About three weeks ago."

"'U die within month.' Have you spoken with him since?"

"Many times. But I've never mentioned that note to him. I've never dared."

"And you don't have the note?"

"No. I said he took it from me."

"You didn't see him throw it away?"

"No."

"Besides letting the President, or the President's office know about the note, have you done anything else about it?"

"I've talked about Professor Loveson in the most general terms to a few people I trust. Without telling them I saw such a note. I got the impression some sort of a game is going on, to harass him. Perhaps I'm taking it too seriously, but I don't think it's very nice, if so. One faculty wit said, 'It's time that old bird had some of his feathers plucked. He's already half-baked.'"

"And what was this half-wit's name?"

She sighed. "Don Carver. I expect he's on your list."

"He is." Cocky had received material, including a list of people to be seen, and rough schedules, from the President's office before Flynn had arrived at Old Records that morning.

"Mr. Flynn?" The voice came from behind his chair. "Are you Mr. Flynn?"

"Yes."

"Telephone, sir. Will you come to the desk?"

"Frank?" Cocky's voice remained cheerful. "Perhaps with my newfound wealth I'll buy you one of those portable telephones."

"Don't you dare."

"Why not? It would make life much easier for me."

"With a phone forever buzzing in my pocket, how would I ever have time to reflect? You're winning enough chess games off me as it is."

"Grover's at CommonWealth Hospital."

"What's he doing there?"

"Got hit by a car, or something."

"Did Grover call you himself?"

"Professor Loveson did."

"Professor— Is he at the hospital, too?"

"I guess he's the one who brought Grover to the hospital. I couldn't understand him very well. He said he thought you would want to know."

"I'll go directly there. Postpone my afternoon schedule, will you, Cocky, old lad?"

"Yes, sir."

"I'll let you know if Grover needs anything from the Sympathy Brigade."

"Should I notify Captain Walsh?"

"Lord, no," said Flynn. "He'll suspect me of stealing Grover's appendix or something."

Dr. Huong waited for him in the foyer.

"I'm sorry," Flynn said. "I must leave you for now. But I will want to talk to you again."

"Anytime," she said.

Going through the door with her, he said, "I'm glad to see Loveson has a friend."

"I am his friend," she said. "I'm not very good at investigating things, not in this century, anyway, I'm focused on the eighteenth century, but please let me help in any way I can."

Flynn said, "There is something you could do for me. Would you prepare me a list of names of people who think they might have been awarded the Samson Chair currently occupied by Professor Loveson if he had retired on time?"

"Of course. I'd only be guessing. Do you think it might be that simple?"

Flynn said, "There's not so much difference among centuries as people might think. 'Vanity, vanity, all is vanity.'"

NINE

———◆———

"Professor Loveson. Sergeant Whelan." Flynn acknowledged both men sitting on a bench in the hall outside the Emergency Room at CommonWealth Hospital. "What are you doing here? You look like two sugar cubes awaiting a hot cup of coffee."

"Coffee." Grover groaned. "Oouuu." He had a sizable bump over his left eye. In his lap he cradled his left wrist in his right hand.

"Nice of you to come along, Inspector Flynn." Loveson had cuts on his right cheekbone and chin. Dried blood remained on his face, shirt, suit coat, and the handkerchief he held in his hand.

"Which of you won?" Flynn asked.

Grover gave Flynn a sour glance. "Not funny, Flynn."

"Richard saved my life," Loveson said.

"'Richard' is it, now?"

"I was crossing the road. I had no idea Richard was anywhere about. Suddenly I felt this whoosh behind me, a big push against my back. Richard picked me up. He ran a few steps with me in his arms. He tripped on the curb. We both sprawled on the sidewalk. Richard broke his wrist, I'm sure. He was unconscious for a few moments, weren't you, Richard?"

Richard winced as he nodded his head.

"And why, 'Richard,' were you playing football with the Professor?"

"Someone was trying to hit him with a car."

"Are you sure?"

"Accelerating zero to sixty on that narrow, short road? The car was aimed right at him."

"I did hear a car accelerating excessively, Inspector."

"Can either of you describe the car?"

"Small," Grover said. "Blue."

"Anything of the license plate?"

"That's why I tripped over the curb," Grover moaned. "I was looking."

"Got nothing of it, eh?"

"If I did, it was knocked out of my head. Oh, my head is killing me."

Flynn looked around the empty waiting room. "So why are you just sitting here?"

"Insurance," Loveson said. "Something about Richard's insurance. They're having to play with the electronic toy to see if it's all right for him to be hurt in the City of Cambridge. Is that right, Richard?"

"But he is hurt in the City of Cambridge," Flynn said.

"I'm an employee of the City of Boston, hurt in the City of Cambridge," Grover said bitterly. "Was I on duty?"

"What difference does that make?" Flynn asked. "You have a concussion and a broken wrist."

Jaws tight, Grover said, "I'm in Cambridge!"

"And you, Professor. I should say your face needs a stitch. Where are you supposed to be under the circumstances? The Harvard Barber College?"

"I insist they take care of Richard first. He's the hero."

"Yes," Flynn said. "You're a hero, Richard. How long have you been waiting?"

"A little over two hours," Loveson said.

Flynn had had to walk a half mile to find a taxi. The police car was not where he and Grover had left it.

The taxi driver told him he had his Ph.D. in art history and did not know where CommonWealth Hospital was. They had arrived there through much inquiry and analysis.

Now Flynn ambled to the desk.

To a woman with a body compacted by a kidney belt standing behind the desk, Flynn said, "I'm Inspector Flynn, of the Boston Police. Perhaps I can help clarify matters. Sergeant Whelan is my assistant. He needs medical attention. He's a hero. He's just saved the life of Professor Louis Loveson."

The woman's eyes flashed. "We put him in the computer!"

"Ah, well, then, that's all right," Flynn said mildly. "Is he getting any better attention there than he is sitting against the wall with a cracked head and broken wrist?"

She shouted, "My God, a mad Irishman! I was married to one once!"

"Um, yes," drawled Flynn. "I can see why he was mad. Do you doubt the sergeant has insurance?"

"We need the Insurance Plan! And the Number!"

"You need a plan," Flynn said, "to set his broken wrist?"

"It's always the soft-talkin' Irish who are the worst! Try to wrap me in charm . . ."

"Perhaps I could give you a telephone number you could call, so you can get his Insurance Plan and his Number—"

"I said, we put him in the computer!"

"The contemporary excuse for all things vile and otherwise unreasonable."

"Right! We need his file! From the computer! Will you go sit down and shut up? Can't you see we're busy?"

There were seven women behind the counter. Three worked computer keyboards, one was on the telephone discussing movies, two chatted about spareribs while eating from cartons of yogurt, and the seventh was busily shouting at Flynn.

In the waiting area, there were only two waiting, Grover and Loveson.

"How can you be busy?" asked Flynn. "Clearly you've already figured out your Going-Out-of-Business strategy."

"Sit down and shut up!"

"I'll do that," Flynn said. "But in some other hospital."

———

"You drove Grover to the hospital in the police car yourself?"

Flynn had taken the car keys from Professor Louis Loveson, found the police car a block away from the hospital, returned, and picked up both men.

"I did." In the front seat beside Flynn, Loveson smiled boyishly. "Richard was very dizzy. I would have rung the siren if I could have found the switch."

"It's not a switch," Flynn lied as a joke. "It's a foot pump."

"Oh." The professor either believed him or did not care.

Grover groaned in the backseat.

"Richard tells me you were to have lunch with Dean Wincomb," Loveson said.

"Yes. I did."

"None of this is his fault, you know."

"None of what?"

Gingerly, Loveson touched his fingertips to his wounded cheekbone. He sighed. He seemed more to be speaking by rote than lecturing. "The American principle of the separation of church and state led to a banning in 1963 of officially sanctioned prayers of any sort in school. That caused confusion and terror in the minds and hearts of American public school teachers, poor dears, who abandoned teaching all culture years ago. We now have generations who don't know a pietà from a pizza, sacred from profane, pride from prejudice, Penelope from Prudence. By the time students get to college they are incapable of cultural perception or discernment."

"That bad, is it?"

"A classic, for instance, is anything, probably originating from popular culture, which has satisfied the needs of many generations. A fad, however big and momentarily indicative, is not its equal. At least, not yet."

"You don't seem much damaged from having been drop-kicked by Grover."

Flynn was driving toward Boston sedately, in consideration for Grover's damaged head.

"Am I dithering?"

"Not the sort of thing usually talked about in police cars."

"What do people usually talk about in police cars?"

"Food. Sex. As elsewhere. Police talk quite a lot about the stupidity of criminals."

"Yes," Loveson said. "Criminal stupidity. And are police compassionate toward the criminally stupid?"

"More than you might think."

"You see? There's not much difference. That woman at the hospital . . ."

"Yes?"

". . . is typical. She perceives the reality of what she is doing, plans and numbers, in the computer rather than what is sitting right in front of her, two men hurting and bleeding. She has given over her human function to an electronic toy, as if to some God."

"The computer as a religious icon?"

"Everywhere you see people bent over it, prayerfully, don't you?"

"Yes."

"We are depositing all our knowledge—at least, our information—in it. Thus we think it omniscient. Even infallible. That woman at the hospital relegated both her perception and thinking abilities to a machine. And don't you find the computer literate suffer from something akin to religious self-righteousness? That they know the truth of how the world works and the computer illiterate do not?"

"Some do."

"Do you believe computers can think, Mr. Flynn?"

"They have no will to survive."

"No self-preservation instinct," Loveson said. "No essentential reason to learn from their experiences. No will at all."

"You should have turned right there," Grover groaned from the backseat.

"Oh. Sorry," Flynn said.

"Speaking of survival." Loveson did not lower his voice. "Not making less of what Richard did—undoubtedly he did save my life—I really believe that that car that came close to me was driven by someone who simply had had too much wine at lunch, or something. Don't you agree, Richard?"

"No. Someone was trying to kill you, Professor."

"Oh, dear." Loveson watched Flynn slide the car into a Police Only parking slot outside the Emergency Room of Boston Barabbas Hospital. "The world will become a very dangerous place indeed if my younger colleagues are right, and the computer leaves us with nothing but our feelings to contend with."

"Speaking of self-preservation," Flynn nearly growled, "you'd better think of exercising a little of it yourself."

Wide-eyed, Loveson stared at Flynn. "Beg pardon?"

"Very soon you need to put on a pretty good Show and Tell, Professor, or, very clearly, you will flunk the grade."

TEN

All school buildings smell of sweaty sneakers. Flynn had learned that. He wasn't sure anyone else knew.

The smell increases as one nears the Physical Education area.

After telling Todd he was there, and that he, Jenny, and Winny should wait for him in the police car after they had showered from sports, Flynn headed for the office of the Cartwright School wrestling coach.

At the hospital, Flynn had waited while Professor Loveson had the skin over his cheekbone stitched and his chin adorned by a butterfly bandage. Grover had his wrist X-rayed and set in a cast. Flynn mocked disappointment when Grover was declared not to need a brain scan. "That picture would be worth few words!" Flynn said.

Then he drove them to their respective homes. He lectured the professor on safety precautions: not to open packages delivered to his home or office; vary his routines, routes, and hours, going between home and office; look both ways before crossing the road . . .

He was having another easy workday.

"Ah, Mr. Flynn!" The Cartwright School wrestling coach, Mr. McLaughlin, was five feet four and weighed a wiry one hundred and thirty-five pounds. "Here for parental reasons, I hope, not police?"

"Betwixt and between." Flynn shook the coach's hand. There was only the one chair in the tiny office, that behind the desk. Both men remained standing. "What do you know of a boy named Billy Capriano?"

"He goes to public school."

"I know."

"I wish he attended Cartwright. I sure could use him on the team. If he keeps on, with proper training, he should have a good crack at State's Championship." The coach smiled broadly. "An A student, too!"

"I understand he quit the wrestling team yesterday."

"He did?" The coach looked disbelieving. "Well, he shouldn't have. Has he an injury?"

"He had a small, you might say, surgical problem over the weekend, resulting in a hole in one earflap, but nothing that should impede his wrestling ability."

Now the coach looked horrified. "No one bit him? I mean, in a wrestling match?"

"No. No one bit him. Someone nailed his ear to a tree."

"'Nailed his ear to a tree'! Good God!"

"Really pinned him, to use wrestling parlance. Have you ever heard of such a thing happening before?"

"Never. Where did this happen?"

"In the cemetery. After dark. Sunday night."

"How did you find him?"

"My daughter, Jenny, happened across him."

"What was Jenny doing in the cemetery after dark Sunday night?"

"Happening across him. Yesterday, he quit his wrestling team. I'm wondering if there is a connection."

"Billy must know who nailed his ear to a tree."

"He won't say."

"Is he afraid of retribution if he tells you?"

"Good guess. I want to know if members of sports teams are apt to intimidate each other in any such manner these days?"

"You mean, to scare him off the team?"

"Something of the sort."

"Unthinkable."

"Not unthinkable," Flynn said. "We're thinking it."

"I've never heard of any such thing. Sure. Boys on the football teams, especially, are apt to hoot at each other when they meet each other with their dates on Friday nights, or something. Grudge fistfights after a game have been known to happen. But intimidate a kid to get off a team because he's excellent? That would be against every rule of good sportsmanship!"

"Oh, yes. It would that. You can't think of any particular boy, or boys, any particular team you might suspect of such unsportsmanlike behavior?"

"No. I've never thought of it. I never want to."

"Do you know Billy?"

"Yes. He, his family, belong to my church. St. Jude's. I've told his parents how much I'd like to have Billy come to Cartwright. For academic reasons, of course." The coach grinned. "I'm not allowed to recruit for the team."

"Are you aware of anything else going on in his life that would cause someone to pin his ear to a tree?"

"No. Fine family. Great kid. Altar boy. I'll stake my life that he doesn't mess with drugs. Or run with a gang. Anything like that. Not Billy."

"My sons say the same thing."

The coach smiled. "The 'Flynn-twin.' It's wonderful watching Randy and Todd work together on the basketball team. They don't even need to look at each other. They always seem to know where each other is. And they cover each other beautifully!"

Flynn laughed with pleasure. "Sure. And I've heard Cartwright has won many points before opposing players learn there are two of 'em."

"Right! At first they think it's the same kid who's every-where at once!"

"But you can't predict what one is going to do from what the other is doing."

"Is that so? I would guess not."

"Can you think of any other reason Billy would quit the wrestling team?"

"No . . ." McLaughlin hesitated. "I believe he has a per-fect record, so far this season. He enjoys the sport. I know he even reads about it. The history of it. I know he works out, even on weekends."

"But . . . ?"

"Nothing. I heard he had a little difficulty with his final match last Thursday. Well, he just wasn't as aggres-sive as he usually is. I was told he drew back, seemed unwilling . . ."

"Did he know the other kid?"

"I don't think so. They were wrestling Newton High School."

"His final match of the day?"

"Yes."

"Something got into him?"

"Something."

"Has his bravery ever been in question?"

"Absolutely not. Not as far as wrestling is concerned. He goes at it like a tiger cub."

"Well, I thank you, Coach McLaughlin."

"Inspector Flynn, if you discover that whoever did this to Billy is connected in any way with this wrestling team or any other, please inform me. I will bring it before the coach's association. Severest disciplinary measures will be taken."

"Indeed I will," Flynn sighed. "I will see severest disciplinary measures are taken."

———

Before dinner, Flynn went into the den and returned a telephone call from Dr. Francine Huong.

"Inspector Flynn? Thanks for calling back. There was a message on my computer from a colleague at the University of California, Berkeley, that an item concerning Dr. Loveson had appeared on the Net. It's really appalling. I can't adequately describe it to you over the phone. I'll make a hard copy of it and bring it to your office in the morning."

"That won't be necessary. How do I get there?"

"Get where?"

"To the right file."

"Are you on the Net?"

"Elsbeth seems to have left the computer running."

"Is Elsbeth your daughter?"

"My wife. Although she'll be pleased you asked."

"Elsbeth Flynn? The poet?"

"The same."

"I adore her poetry. It is so . . . human."

"Elsbeth has every reason to be human."

Dr. Huong gave him the site address.

On Flynn's computer screen there appeared a full figure of Professor Louis Loveson as a skinny old man in a wrinkled suit. Superimposed over his head was the face of Adolph Hitler. On top of all was a mortarboard.

"Nasty," Flynn commented. "Also puerile."

"You see what they've done," Dr. Huong said. "They've taken text from his *Usable Past* and interspersed it with chiding text. Between every line runs a line supposedly reporting what simultaneously was occurring in the history of Woman—"

"As opposed to Man," Flynn added.

"Jews. Africans. Asians. Throughout the text. There are reams of it."

Flynn scrolled ahead.

Throughout the text were cartoons of Louis Loveson. He was running around and around in the center of a maze.

"Pointedly disjointed," Flynn observed.

"How dastardly unfair," Dr. Huong said. "Inspector Flynn," she continued. "You may not have noticed. I am a woman. Also an Asian American."

Reading, Flynn said, "I see."

"Dr. Louis Loveson's work is monumental. It will stand always. In fact, his work remains the most inclusive such work in the canon. It is perhaps the best fact-based work on historical cause and effect." Her voice changed. "This is so unfair!"

"And we have no way of discovering who published this on the Net, do we?"

"None."

"Do you spot anything, Dr. Huong, which might give you a clue as to who perpetrated this?"

"No. It could be anybody anywhere in the world. Possibly even someone not associated with a university."

"But someone with a motive, surely?"

Dr. Huong said, "You surf the Net enough you'll find tons of garbage motivated by nothing but sheer nastiness."

"That's true. But this was a lot of work."

Dr. Huong said, "There was a day when published academic comment was required to have some imprimatur guaranteeing responsibility."

"But wasn't that considered stifling?" Flynn continued to scan the texts. "Didn't that frequently lead, in fact, to exclusivity?"

She sighed into the phone. "Of course. But humans' own sense of responsibility hasn't matured enough to let them play fairly with these toys."

"Possibly true," said Flynn. "But can a sense of responsibility develop without freedom? Mustn't one first see the need for responsibility?"

"My, my," she said. "Yes. I suppose that's what Louie Loveson would say. Still, this makes me bloody angry!"

"I gather from the way Dr. Loveson disdains the computer, he does not use one himself?"

"No. In his more humorous moments, he refers to the computer as a Ouija board."

"So he will not see this?"

"Not unless someone sits down with him, puts his knees against his, and shows it to him. Surely, I won't."

"Your colleague in California, Dr. Huong, who notified you this garbage is on the Net . . . Could he or she possibly be the perpetrator? Perhaps using you as a way of getting Loveson to see this ordure?"

"No. Absolutely not. I've talked with her since I've read this. She's as upset as I am. We're discussing putting up a protest."

"Will you?"

"I don't know. What do you think?"

"Thank you very much for showing me this, Dr. Huong. What I think is that the best answer to a rude noise may be silence."

———

At dinner, Winny opened his gambit. "Da?"

"Yes, Winny?"

"We'd all like to talk to you about having a family television."

"We have a family television." Flynn touched his forkful of meatloaf to the catsup on the side of his plate. "It's in our bedroom."

"Highly restrictive," Todd said.

Randy was not at table.

"You're welcome to look at it anytime," Elsbeth said.

"Sure," Todd scoffed. "With you two in and out."

"We mean a family television," Winny said. "A big one. Perhaps in the living room? Facing the couch? Like other families have."

"What would we do with the piano?" Flynn asked.

"We could put the television on top of the piano," Winny said.

Flynn's groan was drowned out by a jet airplane taking off from Logan Airport low over the house.

The family was used to such pauses in their conversation.

Finally, Elsbeth said, "Good. The piano as a television stand."

"A big television," Winny amended.

"Baby grand piano. Big television." Elsbeth said, "Mr. Johann Sebastian Bach would be so glad we've discovered a new use for his well-tempered clavier." She nodded her head in agreement. "He said the piano was more versatile than we knew."

"We need a television in the kitchen, too," Todd said. "So Mother can stay more in touch with the world."

"Good!" Elsbeth exclaimed. "I have a new recipe for a broccoli pie I would have made already except it takes such a long time."

"If we had all these televisions all over the house," Flynn asked, "what would you look at on it that you're not looking at now?"

"I could watch the daytime talk shows," Elsbeth said. "Listen to vulgar people blame everyone else for their being so vulgar."

Shrewdly, Winny answered, "The news."

"Ah, yes," answered Flynn. "The Making News Shows. Offering only the news of which they have videotape."

"Some of them are thoughtful," Jenny said.

"Ah, yes," answered Flynn. "Extrapolatory News. If two horses fell in the mud two years ago and three horses fell in the mud last year, by the year 2075, 56,000 horses will fall in the mud."

"Situation comedies," Winny said. "All the kids in school talk about them and I don't know what they're talking about because I have to sit here every night at family dinner eating meatloaf, listening to Jenny scare me about algebra. And then do the dishes!"

"Ah, yes," answered Flynn. "Sitcoms, most of which seem to derive their comedy from sexual-identity confusion."

"Laughter alleviates such pain," Elsbeth said.

"There should be no pain in what we are," countered Flynn. "Or, more precisely, in what others aren't."

"I rather like the mysteries," Jenny put in.

"Ah, yes," answered Flynn. "Those dramas which insensitize us to violence while proving over and over and over that people of substance and accomplishment, too, have Achilles' heels, and thus are no better than the rest of us."

Todd said, "You've probably never even seen the late-night comics."

"Ah, yes," answered Flynn. "Those who tar their superiors with a very thick brush indeed. Someone in the public eye slips on a throw rug and forever after is an object of derision concerning his clumsiness, inner-ear problems, drunkenness, or worse. Innuendo carried to the point where it shatters on the rock of poor taste."

Todd slapped his hand on the table. "Sports!"

"Ah, yes," answered Flynn. "An hour's game played out over four hours interspersed with commercials making beer-drinking, snack-consuming and pill-taking seem the route to good health and great athleticism."

"You like sports?" Elsbeth asked her children. "Then play sports. You'll get more oxygen. Anyone want more meatloaf?"

"Da," Todd insisted. "The Talmud, Old Testament, New Testament, and Koran are not all there is to life!"

"No," agreed Flynn. "There are Eastern and Western ideas you haven't encountered yet."

Bravely, Winny asked, "Are we going to get a big television for the living room, or not?"

Answered Flynn: "Not."

ELEVEN

The next morning, while the car was warming up, Flynn stood in the driveway, sniffing the air, looking at the partly cloudy sky, the birds on the tree branch no one had yet scared away by shooting one.

He watched a jet airplane fly low over the house on its way to somewhere Flynn was glad he was not going.

The roar of the jet engines did not scare the birds from the tree branch.

Carrying his sports/books bag under his arm like a football, Randy was the first to come out of the house and down the back steps.

"Well?" his father asked.

"Seeing he quit the wrestling team, Billy has to work in the family butcher shop every day after school. He went straight there from school. I talked to him a few minutes. I went in to buy a candy bar."

"Did you ask him why he quit the wrestling team?"

"He said he was tired of wrestling."

"Do you believe him?"

"No. And he gave me some nonsense about wanting to work to save up to buy a car." Randy shrugged. "He's only fourteen. He has a cut of some kind on his ear."

"Yes."

"He went home with his father shortly after the store closed at six. They rode in a car. I jogged."

"Much healthier for you, I'm sure."

"I guess they had supper. He left the house about seven-fifteen. He went to the cemetery. Jenny was waiting for him there."

"I see."

"They sat on a tombstone and talked for about an hour."

"What did they say?"

"I didn't listen."

"You couldn't hear them?"

"I didn't listen!"

"All right."

"They kissed hello. They kissed good-bye. Sitting on the tombstone together they held hands. Is that what you wanted to know?"

Flynn shook his head no.

"Jenny gave him something. A little box. I think it was an earring. Anyway, then she played with his ear for a while—where I had observed the cut? He said, 'Ow,' a few times. They giggled. Then they sat and talked some more. He touched his ear several times."

Flynn wondered if Jenny now knew why Billy's ear had been nailed to the tree.

He doubted it.

"Billy went straight home. I watched the house until his

bedroom light went off about ten-fifteen. I waited a while, to make sure he did not come out again, even through the back door. Then I came home." Randy yawned. "Do you want Todd and me to continue watching him?"

"No. The boy is as pure as driven snow."

"That's good." A pained expression came over Randy's face. "Da, I really don't like spying on my sister."

Flynn's big hand cupped the back of Randy's head. "That's good."

———

"Good morning, Cocky!" In his office Flynn went directly to the chessboard near the fireplace and moved a black knight.

Cocky smiled. "I thought you'd do that."

He moved a white pawn.

"Ah!" Flynn studied the board. "Now that gives me a problem, doesn't it?"

"I have your adjusted schedule. How's Grover?"

"Broken left wrist. Concussion. A few blue marks on his face. An undeniable heroic gleam in his eye."

"He called saying he wasn't coming in today."

"Taking a sick-out day, is he?" Flynn studied his schedule. "Well deserved. It's not everybody who has picked up a seventy-six-year-old Harvard professor and made a field goal with him."

"On your desk is a file concerning Lieutenant Detective John Kurt."

"Ah, yes." Sitting at his desk, Flynn opened the file. "Observation?"

"He has a remarkable record of convictions."

"Further observation?"

"I'm not sure, but it almost could be said he's never arrested anyone white."

"Ah! That's the way it is, is it?"

"I'm not sure. Also Mr. John Roy Priddy's office asks that you call him."

"I see." Cocky had relayed many such messages from No Name Zero.

Never had Cocky asked about John Roy Priddy.

Somehow he had understood he ought not.

"He said just to call the Pittsburgh number. Tea?"

"Good man!"

Flynn waited until Cocky had left the office before dialing the phone.

"Thirteen," he said into the phone. "Zero."

Instantly, John Roy Priddy's voice said, "Good morning, Flynn."

"Sir."

Flynn knew John Roy Priddy could be anywhere in the world, at any time in his day or night. John Roy hated sleep. He hated the accompanying nightmares.

"How's Elsbeth?"

"Fine, sir."

"Todd?"

"Fine."

"Randy?"

"Fine."

John Roy seldom talked to Flynn without asking for each member of his family individually.

"Jenny?"

"Fine."

"Winny?"

"Fine."

"Jeff?"

"Rollicking."

"That's good. Louis Loveson?"

"Not so good."

"I hope I didn't put you in line for just a baby-sitting job with him, Flynn."

"I'm not baby-sitting him. In fact, for some reason, I'm having one of the easiest weeks of my life."

"It's just that the President of Harvard expressed concern to me about him, and, luckily enough, you're in Boston . . ."

"Was Loveson a professor of yours?"

"Yes. I'm personally very fond of him."

"He's not cooperating even slightly."

"He has his own mind."

"Indeed he has. He can't deny his colleagues are giving him the cold shoulder. That much is obvious. He denies he's being threatened in any way."

"All respects due the President," N. N. Zero posited slowly, "Loveson isn't really being threatened, is he?"

"His ex–teaching assistant, Dr. Francine Huong, says that three weeks ago she saw a childish note threatening his life, and, within the month. Loveson grabbed the note away from her. He would not answer her questions about it. In fact, he expressed anger at her having seen it at all. I personally have seen no such written threats. When I was with him in his apartment night before last, I believe he received a threatening phone call. He denied that."

"I saw the attack upon him and his work on the Net yesterday."

"Yes. He demonizes the computer. Or those who relegate their personalities to it."

"I had a great-grandaunt who thought the radio caused lightning storms."

"It doesn't?"

"What's causing this assault upon Louie Loveson, Flynn?"

"Well, it is the beginning of a new century, isn't it?"

"Could you possibly be less precise?"

Flynn chuckled. "I'll try. Loveson seems to believe these generations, his junior colleagues, have thrown away our usable past. Without any such past, he sees chaos in our future."

"Try our present," Priddy said.

"He believes teachers should act as navigators."

"That assumes we came from somewhere and presumes that we are going somewhere."

"Not a novel idea."

"Flynn, isn't this all just academic nonsense? The junior colleagues having a bit of nasty fun with the old boy?"

"I'm not sure. Are you?"

"I think maybe that nonsense on the Net yesterday was there because technology permits it to be there. Anonymously. Haven't you ever wanted to assault a superior anonymously, Flynn?"

"Assault you, John Roy? Beggar the thought! Of course

there have been a few times I've found myself in uncomfortable places in the world not immediately sure what precisely I was doing there . . ."

"Have you ever once failed to figure it out?"

". . . those times my heartbeat reached a thousand and two to the minute."

"Flynn, do you believe Louie Loveson is in physical danger?"

"Yesterday afternoon, my sergeant-assistant felt he had to scoop Loveson up in his arms in the middle of a road and drop him on the sidewalk to avoid his being run over by an accelerating vehicle."

"Oh."

"The sergeant definitely thought the driver of the vehicle was trying to kill the professor."

"What did Loveson think?"

"He thought the driver probably had too much wine with his lunch."

"What do you think?"

"I think either is possible."

"I shouldn't have asked. I guess there's enough reason for you to keep a watch on Louie Loveson."

"It is much harder to protect the alleged victim without his cooperation."

"If almost being run over yesterday, after notes threatening his life—if there were such notes—didn't wring cooperation out of him, nothing will."

"He does seem determined to hold his flag all by himself," Flynn said. "Up high."

TWELVE

"To be as frank as I can," Flynn said in Dr. Bryce Fine's office, "Professor Louis Loveson may or may not be receiving threatening notes and threatening telephone calls. You saw that attack upon him on the Net yesterday?"

Behind his desk, Professor Fine answered simply, "Yes."

"Someone may or may not have tried to run over him in a car yesterday afternoon."

Sitting slumped sideways to his desk, Fine snorted. "With all your 'may's and 'may not's,' I suspect the President has asked you to watch over old Louie. Correct? I'm not surprised old Louie has friends in high places. I've noticed your name in the newspapers, Inspector Flynn. I guess he deserves special attention. Seventy-six years old . . . Still, what may or may not be happening to Louie Loveson is nothing more or less than indicative."

"Beg pardon?"

"Forgive me, I'm tired. I've just finished lecturing. Sherry?"

"No, thanks."

Fine poured from a decanter on a bookcase a step from his desk. "Lecturing is a great deal more difficult than it used to be."

Under Dr. Fine's good tweed jacket was a partially buttoned cardigan sweater. He wore a soft necktie. He carried perhaps twenty-five pounds he didn't need. His thick black hair was graying.

"One just can't plow ahead and say what one is saying anymore. One must bob and weave, bob and weave." He swung his glass, not enough to spill the sherry. "Reach out, up, down, genuflect to this bit of political correctness, that bit. Things used to be understood. Taken for granted. 'Everyone must pass in his paper next Friday.' A simple statement. 'Everyone must pass in his or her paper next Friday.' I'll be damned if I'll follow current trends and say, 'Everyone must pass in their paper next Friday!'" He shot his sherry down his throat. "Sorry. It's just that when I get done, having to take two steps sideways for every step forward, I have no idea what it is I've just said! Or if I've said anything. And I'm tired! Sure you won't have some sherry?"

"No, thanks."

Fine poured himself more. Sitting down at his desk, he sipped from his glass more slowly. "Not to worry. I guess I'm at the age where I shouldn't care so much. I do my job as much as I'm permitted. And go home." He smiled. "Working on the Great American Novel. Well, I'm trying to write a novel on current university life."

"Good luck."

"It's balderdash, of course. What percentage of American professors are trying to write the definitive novel on contemporary university life? Trying to understand it?"

"Is that what novel writing is?"

"Having spent so much time in the contemporary university, unfortunately I find myself deconstructing before constructing." He laughed ruefully. "Reminds me of the composer who decomposed before he composed. Wouldn't leave much, would it?"

"More to the point . . ."

"In a way, I respect old Loveson. He still cares. He still believes Truth is to be pursued. At seventy-six, he's still in there fighting."

Flynn cleared his throat. "More to the point . . ."

"There is a point?"

"For the moment, let's pretend there is," Flynn said, "seeing we're in a room alone together."

"All this didn't start with the destruction of the Harvard Freshman Union in 1996, you know, Flynn."

"I'm sure not."

"Besides the President of Harvard University, and other distinguished personages of course, Dr. Loveson also taught Theodore John Kaczynski, didn't he? Class of 1962."

Flynn's eyebrows shot up. "Is that what this is all about? The Unabomber?"

"Kaczynski had a valid point, you know. Is Mankind—sorry, Personkind—better or worse off since the industrial and technological revolutions? Mao asked the same question. He thought it best to keep a billion Chinese occupied at manual labor than to take those first steps over the threshold in which human beings begin to become superfluous." Fine finished his sherry and smiled. "Of course

Kaczynski's manner of addressing the problem, however dramatic, was not the best. I've always thought his insanity was that he thought himself some sort of a martyr, for asking the unpopular obvious."

"More to the point . . ."

"Yes?"

"Are you aware of any person or persons who feel so strongly about Dr. Loveson they sincerely might be threatening his life? For example, have you any clue as to who put that trashing of his work on the Net yesterday?"

"Louie Loveson has become the antithesis of current academic trends. He insists in believing in the linear. He believes that what he calls civilization cannot continue without at least some people having a solid grounding in the historical, cultural, political, and scientific foundations of what he calls Our Society. In 1914, 82 percent of colleges required a math course; 86 percent required science. By 1993, the percentages had fallen to 12 percent and 34 percent. In 1914, 76 percent of the colleges required a philosophy course; by 1993, only 4 percent. Need I go on? Am I being didactic? You asked me to describe my opinion of Louie Loveson's present difficulties. He who bucks the trend is apt to be unpopular."

"To the point of someone wanting to run him over with a car?"

"Louie Loveson's point is that those who make decisions ought to have a thorough background in decision making. This leads to at least two questions. Who gets to make the decisions for society? Some elitist group taught by Louie Loveson?"

"And the second question?"

Dr. Bryce Fine hesitated. He mentally framed the question before posing it.

"If one disagrees with the person who insists one must have an education in making decisions, what does one bring to the decision to kill that person?"

———

The instant Flynn rang the front doorbell, somewhere within the house a pane of glass smashed.

He drew back.

He wasn't sure he should ring the doorbell again.

He had made a lunch by stopping at a convenience store and buying a quarter pound of cheddar cheese and a half quart of orange juice. He ate and drank as he drove to the small stucco home of Assistant Professor Donald Carver in Arlington.

He had needed to climb two flights of concrete steps through unkempt crabgrass and bits of glass, aluminum, cardboard to get to the front door.

The second time he rang the doorbell a young girl screamed.

The front door opened. The storm door was pushed out.

A man wearing earphones sideways on his head said, "Inspector Flynn?"

"Yes." Flynn entered. "Dr. Carver?"

The man caught the wire dangling from his head. "I wouldn't have heard the doorbell, if Charley hadn't broken the window from the sunroom."

"How fortunate," Flynn drawled.

Carver led the way into what had been originally designed as a parlor.

Central to the room, a television blared. On the back wall glowed a computer screen. Next to it was a stereo turned on, but soundless.

Apparently Carver had been sitting at the computer screen while listening to the stereo through earphones.

Shaking his wire in his fist, Carver hummed loudly the theme of "Ode to Joy."

Broken glass from a sunporch window was on a section of the living-room floor.

Otherwise, the room, including the single worn couch and the glass-topped coffee table, was strewn with plastic toys, most of them broken, children's socks, underpants, other articles of clothing, plus some of the vast quantities of paper and cardboard advertisements sold by the fast-food chains. There were also eleven empty cans of soft drinks, and two empty wine bottles visible in the room; a half-empty bottle of beer was next to the computer keyboard.

"I see you were expecting me," Flynn said.

"Yes . . . The office of the President called . . . I have to work here today. Charley and Bess were sent home from school. My wife works, of course."

Carver was shoving stuff from one cushion of the couch to another. "Beer?"

Two men, one light, one dark, dressed only in what appeared to be metal loincloths, each armed with a broad sword, poised to try to kill each other, were frozen on the computer screen.

"Sorry to disturb your work," Flynn said.

A young girl's voice sounded from somewhere in the house. "Charley! Bastard!"

Carver turned his computer chair around to face the

couch. Indicating the couch with the beer bottle he invited Flynn to sit.

Carver followed Flynn's eyes. He, too, looked at the computer screen. "Popular culture."

"Is it?" Flynn asked.

And on the television screen, all in a row, sat six huge humans in big wigs and tight dresses. A line running at the bottom of the screen identified them as U.S. AND CANADIAN TRANSVESTITE WRESTLING TEAMS.

A mustached man in a slim gray suit approached one after another with a phallic-shaped traveling microphone. He kept shouting, "But you don't really mean that!"

"I do!" one of the wrestlers insisted through cherry-colored lipstick. "I'll twist his head off right here, right now, for all to see!" The person tugged at his bra. "I'll throw his head into the audience! They can use it for a football!"

The audience gasped.

"But you don't really mean that!"

Bringing the mascara around his eyes closer together, the person said, "I do!"

"I called Wincomb," Carver said. "He said you're hot on the trail of whoever is upsetting old Loveson's feathers."

The television said: "Bastard!"

"I'm a bastard? You're a shmuck!"

"Bastard!"

Somewhere in the house, the young girl's voice screamed, "Charley bastard bastard bastard!"

Flynn stood up from the couch. "If you don't mind . . ." He turned off the television.

"About time someone put Loveson down." Carver

sucked at his beer bottle. "I use that expression in the veterinarian sense."

Flynn sat again on his square of couch cushion. "You mean, kill him."

Carver shrugged.

Flynn's ears told him some heavy, square, wooden object fell down the stairs from the second floor.

"Has an actual crime been committed against Loveson yet?" Carver asked.

"I'm not sure," Flynn said. "I don't think much about crime, per se."

"But you're a policeman!" Carver giggled.

"What is your criticism of Professor Loveson?" Flynn asked. "In one hundred words or less?"

"He's a liar."

"A liar?"

"Dishonest. A hypocrite, anyway."

A boy of about seven presented himself in the living room. He was barefooted. He wore baggy green shorts that reached below his knees. His T-shirt read: LIFE SUCKS. His skin was sallow, his eyes sullen. He had more hair on one side of his head than the other.

"Charley, my friend." His father held out a hand to him. "I want you to do me a favor."

To Flynn, the boy looked as if he were about to explode with unhappiness.

"Would you please get the broom and the dustpan and clean up this glass for me? I'll appreciate it."

The boy looked at the broken glass in the corner of the room.

"If you do a good job, I'll give you a candy bar later."

"There is no later." The boy turned on the television set.

A girl about nine came into the room. She was dressed in a red nylon bra and bikini. Her toenails were painted red.

Flynn dug his fingers into his stomach. When he mixed orange juice with cheddar cheese for lunch he did not know he would see such sights this afternoon.

"Charley's a bastard," she notified her father.

Carver laughed. "Now, Bess. Technically, you do not know that."

"In what way," Flynn asked over the roar of applause from the television, "do you consider Professor Loveson a hypocrite?"

"He lies to protect himself. To protect a dead world. He insists there's a logic—what, God given?—some sort of a line of reasoning throughout history that leads to our present state of perfection. His perfection. Our imperfection."

"Does he indeed?"

Bess had darted out of the room.

"Embedded in everything Loveson has ever written, ever taught is racism, anti-Semitism, sexism."

"Is that so?"

"Sure. The superiority of the white male. He's still trying to justify all the evils of history as some sort of intellectual, spiritual progress. He ignores the destitution of all the oppressed peoples this so-called progress has caused."

On his bare feet, Charley walked on the broken glass.

"He's defending the indefensible establishment." Carver noted what his son was doing, but continued what he was saying. "He still believes in an elite, the idea of a group of people taught to make and exercise value judgments for all of us, for society. Needless to say, these navigators, these decision makers, this elite is comprised of only people taught by Louie Loveson, Ph.D., squatter in the Samson Chair at Harvard University, Queen's Knight, and et cetera ad nauseam!"

On the television ran a commercial for pills to take an hour before eating, to avoid excess stomach acid.

Flynn asked, "Dr. Loveson was your professor while you were an undergraduate at Harvard?"

"Yes. So I know what I'm talking about." Carver waved his beer bottle. "God! How we swallowed that stuff . . . at first."

"You are a white male, aren't you?"

"My great-grandmother was an Indian princess."

"Oh, God," Flynn groaned. "A Cherokee, I'm sure."

"How did you know?"

Bess came into the room. She hit her brother on the back of his head with a saucepan.

Dripping blood from his feet, yowling, Charley fled to the back of the house.

Carver laughed. "Bonk!"

"My God, man!" Flynn stood up and snapped off the television set. "Will you curb your children?"

"'Curb'? Like you curb a dog?" His face reddened. "You mean, admonish my children?"

"For starters," Flynn said.

"I have no more right to admonish my children than they have to admonish me," Carver stated.

"Then what in God's name are you doing here?"

"I'm not here in God's name, copper. Neither are you. There is no authority in this world, or above it. And that includes you!"

Standing, hands behind his back, Flynn said, "You studied at Harvard, one of the world's most prestigious universities?"

"Yes."

"You studied under Professor Loveson?"

"Yes."

"That gives you the authority to teach?"

"I don't teach! Not as you use the word, anyway."

"What do you do with your students?"

"We discuss. Sometimes we arrive at a consensus."

"Then why do they need you?"

"They don't, really." Carver placed his empty beer bottle on his computer table. "Maybe they need a room to gather in, on cold days. A reading list. Maybe someone to knock the certainty out of them."

Bess ran shrieking through the room.

Charley chased her with a raised kitchen carving knife.

Flynn said, "Stop it, you two!"

Carver caught Charley's free arm. "Whoa, whoa, old chum. Time out!"

Carver held firmly on to the wriggling boy's arm.

The boy shouted, "I'm going to kill her!" He tried to tug his arm free.

"Time-out," Carver said. "Now I want you to really think about killing your sister."

"Good God," said Flynn. "Vandalism. Aggravated assault. Attempted murder. And you call a time-out!"

"Maybe you're just a little bit tired?" Carver suggested to his son. "Would you like some more Chinese food? Chicken Hoi Toi? You like Chicken Hoi Toi."

There was a crash from the back of the house. Flynn's ears suggested the clatter was from a drawer full of knives, forks, and spoons.

Carver looked up at Flynn. "And I do not appreciate your trying to correct my children!"

"Beggar the thought!"

"Are we done?" Carver asked Flynn.

"What color is your car?" Flynn asked.

"Brown."

"Your wife's car?"

"Blue."

"Where were you early afternoon yesterday?"

"Playing hoops."

"You mean, basketball without the rules." Flynn had difficulty seeing Louis Loveson engaged in such an activity. "This recreational use of your computer . . ."

Carver held Charley lightly by his wrist. "Do me a favor, Charley? Drop the knife?"

"Is it because recently you have spent hours feeding script and cartoons regarding Louis Loveson onto the Net?"

"I have no idea what you mean." Carver smiled.

Charley dropped the knife onto the floor.

With his hand thus freed, he slapped his father hard across the face.

"Oh, Charley!" Carver dropped both his arms to his sides. His eyes watered. "I'm so sorry!" He looked at the boy. "I'm so sorry to have corrected you!"

Charley darted toward the back of the house.

"My God, man. Don't you see what you're doing?" Flynn looked around the room. He particularly looked at the small bloodied footprints. "Chaos!"

Carver smiled. "We think they're both creative."

"You said your wife works. What does she do for a living?"

"She's a child psychologist." Yawning, Carver stood up. "The school's a bit upset with us, because we don't want to put Bess and Charley on Ritalin just yet."

Flynn opened the front door himself. Suddenly wild electronic music was blaring from the back of the house.

At the door, Carver said, "If there were a God, I'd pray to her you don't have children, Copper Flynn. They'd probably grow up just like you."

THIRTEEN

———◆———

Elsbeth was right, of course. The sign over the butcher shop in Winthrop said, in big letters, CAPRIANOS' MEATS.

Still, Flynn had seen the name somewhere else, recently, in an odder context.

He wished he could remember where.

"Good afternoon, Mr. Flynn!" The big-chested man behind the counter wiped his hands on his white apron. A finger was missing from his left hand.

"Good afternoon, William. How's the family?"

"Still cookin' along," William said. "Cookin' along."

"Who could ask for anything more?"

Flynn had spotted Billy Capriano, also in an apron, stacking cans from a box in one of the aisles.

Billy had glanced at Flynn when he came in.

And looked away.

"Do you have a leg of lamb?" Flynn asked.

"Why? Did you lose one?" William guffawed at his own pleasantry. "We have a nice leg of lamb for you. Would you like me to dress it for you?"

"Dress a leg of lamb?"

"In sheer nylon," William suggested. "Or maybe a black net stocking would be more to your taste? We'll throw in the brass anklet inscribed 'Feeling Sheepish,' for free."

"You're beginning to make me lose my taste for a leg of lamb, William."

"Naked leg of lamb coming right up, Mr. Flynn. I should have known you'd prefer it that way."

As William went into the huge freezer, his brother Tony came out.

"Hey, Inspector Flynn! Send any bad guys away for a vacation today?"

"Not yet," Flynn said. "But I have my eye on your brother."

"That's good," Tony said. "Before you send him to prison, make sure he has a new tennis racket and enough tennis balls to last a while." He said to the woman he was serving, "Here's your crown roast, Mrs. Featherstone-haugh. Isn't it a beauty?"

So, Flynn mused to himself: Tony Capriano thinks we police are soft on crime.

William washed the leg of lamb in a big sink behind the counter before wrapping it.

Flynn said, "I see you have Billy working here now."

"Oh, oh," William said. "Are you going to charge us with violating child labor laws?"

"First tell me how much the lamb is a pound."

"We're not violating Capriano labor laws." William lifted the lamb onto clean white wrapping paper. "My Daddy had me working here when I was three years old. Sweeping floors. Billy did, too."

"But look how you turned out."

"Billy's been handy with a knife since he was nine."

"I thought he was on the school wrestling team. Doesn't he need to practice after school?"

"His choice. He quit Monday. Came home. Told me at supper he wanted to work in the market after school. I was some surprised. Usually we only use him during school vacations. Boy, was the coach some mad! He's called me a dozen times, if once."

"There wasn't a discipline problem?"

William looked puzzled at Flynn. "Why would you ask that?"

"The kids have told me how much he likes wrestling, how good he is at it."

"Billy's a discipline problem, all right," his father said. "He's got too much of it, to my mind. Gets himself up in the morning, cleans his room before going to school, never misses a day, does his homework as soon as he gets home. He spends his free time either working out or reading these books of history so huge you could never grill 'em. You think he might have the makings of a history teacher, Mr. Flynn?"

"Maybe. If we ever decide again that we have a history."

"You know what he does when I say, 'Billy, relax a little, take off your sneakers, look at this movie on TV?' He says, 'Okay, Dad,' and goes out and runs twelve miles. To him, that's relaxing! Discipline problem? I should slap him down! Anything else, Mr. Flynn?"

"I'll go find some of that excellent mint sauce you sell."

"Okay." William lifted the wrapped leg of lamb over the meat case and handed it to Flynn. "You'll find some down there near where Billy is working."

Leg of lamb under his arm, Flynn said to the boy kneeling in the aisle, "Good afternoon, Billy."

"Hi, Mr. Flynn."

Billy did not really look up at him. He continued stamping and stacking cans of tomato paste.

"How's the ear?"

"Fine."

"What's that I see gleaming from it?"

"An earring. Jenny gave me an earring. Fill up the hole. Make it less obvious."

"I've never seen an earring placed so high up in an ear before."

"Whoever pierced my ear didn't think I'd use the hole for an earring."

Looking down at the boy's head, Flynn noticed how neatly Billy's brown hair was cut, combed.

"The kids all think it's cool." Billy chuckled. "A few of my buddies want to have their ears pierced in the same place."

"Trendsetting, are you? I worry the brass will turn your ear green."

"It's gold."

"Is it? Jenny must be getting too much allowance. I'll see about that!"

Below the rolled-up sleeves of his white shirt, Billy's forearms were remarkably well formed, muscular, for a fourteen-year-old.

Warmly, Flynn liked Jenny's loving him.

"Are you ready to tell me yet who pinned you to the tree, Billy?"

Looking up, the boy's brown eyes were steady in Flynn's. "If I was willing to tear my ear off rather than tell you, Mr. Flynn, do you think I'll tell you now? Or ever?"

"I guess not."

Billy's attention returned to tomato paste.

"Why did you quit the wrestling team, Billy?"

"I want to work in the store. Make some money."

"No one believes that."

Billy shrugged.

"There's a rumor around that in your last match last Thursday, you didn't try your hardest."

"I didn't need to." Billy tried to hide a slight smile. "In a way, I tried my hardest."

What did that smile mean?

Flynn said, "I always believe a person should do what he's best at—as long as it's not illegal, immoral, or slothful."

Billy said, "I'm very good at stacking tomato cans."

"That you are," Flynn said. "Yes. I can see that. Where's your bottled mint sauce?"

———

"Woe!" Randy came into the kitchen where Flynn was trying to make room in the refrigerator for the leg of lamb. "There's a real belt-in-the-belly waiting for you in the living room, Da."

"What's a 'belt-in-the-belly'?"

Of course, Flynn had heard the doorbell.

Randy placed his forearms where his belly would be, if he had one. "Woe! A real gorgeous lady . . . She's so gorgeous, she makes me wobble."

Flynn closed the refrigerator door. "You've gone queer all over, have you?"

"No." Randy groaned. "Not queer."

"Did she give a name?"

"Dr. Huong. Oh, Huong!" He pretended to lurch against the kitchen counter. "Huong!" He said it as if it were a musical sound, perhaps of a temple bell. "Huong . . ."

"Bless your raging hormones, lad." Flynn patted him on the head. "Sure, I hope we get you through school before they carry you off to prowl the alleys like a tomcat."

"Huong," Randy said.

"Good afternoon, Dr. Huong," Flynn said in the living room. In a trim beige suit and ruffled shirt collar, clear eyes, healthy skin, Dr. Huong indeed was gorgeous.

"Hope I haven't upset things by dropping in at your home, Inspector Flynn."

"Not at all. You've just confirmed, for the second time this afternoon, my conviction that my children have very good taste."

Flynn heard someone go up the stairs.

"Was that your son who answered the door?"

"He used to be. Suddenly he's just a jar of jelly."

Todd came into the room. "Hello," he said.

Francine said to him, "You don't look like a jar of jelly to me."

"What?"

"This is Todd," Flynn said. "Dr. Huong."

"We've just met," Dr. Huong said.

Todd said, "Never. I'd remember. Excuse me. I need the new bow."

Francine looked the boy up and down. "Where are you thinking of wearing it?"

"What?" In a corner of the room, Todd knelt on one knee and took a bow out of a violin case.

Big-eyed, Randy came into the room.

Francine looked from one to the other. "Oh, I see." She said to Randy, "You're the jar of jelly."

"Yes, ma'am."

"Can't you two mark your shorts, or something? At least wear different colors?"

Randy stuttered, "School uniform."

"I should have realized," Francine said. "I guess I've read about you two."

"You have?" Randy was entranced.

"References," Francine said. "In some of your mother's poems. You're 'Double Love,' aren't you?"

"We are?" Todd asked absently. "Da, Jenny took my resin!"

Flynn said, "More commonly known as the 'Flynn-twin.'"

"Is it fun," Francine asked the boys, "being a twin?"

They started their routine.

"Only when I'm Randy," Todd said.

"And when I'm Todd," said Randy.

"But when I'm Todd," said Todd.

"And I'm Randy . . ."

"Then we each have to pull on our own pants," Todd concluded, for this time. He left the room calling, "Jennifer! Give me back my resin, or I'll pluck your eye out and put it in Mama's fruit salad!"

"Do sit," Flynn said.

Randy sat, too. Agog.

"Lovely home." Francine looked around the living room, the baby grand piano, Flynn's cello nestled in the curve of it, the music stands, the three violin cases. "Lovely family."

Flynn said, "This afternoon someone said to me, 'If there were a God, I'd pray to her you don't have children, Copper Flynn. They'd probably grow up just like you.'"

"A fate worse than death," Randy muttered. "I'm hoping to grow up a head of lettuce."

"I'm sorry anyone would say that to you," Francine said. "Who was it?"

"Actually, your colleague, Don Carver."

"Is Don guilty . . ." Francine kept her eyes on Flynn's face. ". . . of anything?"

"Yes," Flynn said. "I'm thinking of having him charged with child abuse."

Francine settled her large, soft-leather purse in her lap. "As you asked, Inspector, I inquired about the Samson Chair, currently held by Professor Loveson."

"Yes?"

"What I understand is that Louie is to be the last holder of that chair, as such."

"How can that be? Aren't such chairs usually endowed forever?"

"Usually. The endowment for the Samson Chair, however prestigious, is pitifully small. In fact, the chair's prestige mostly has derived, until recently, that is, from the fact that Louie Loveson holds it."

"What will happen to the endowment?"

"Apparently it will be folded in with some other endowment, possibly for a chair in Women's Studies, possibly for Gay and Lesbian Studies."

"How very compartmental."

"Isn't it."

Flynn looked at Randy. At first, Flynn thought Randy was being politely quiet. Then he saw that Randy was so agog staring at Francine Huong that he wasn't hearing a word.

"So," Flynn said, "at the moment, no obvious person feels deprived by Louie Loveson's maintaining the Samson Chair, or deriving what little income there is from it."

"No. The Samson Chair will be retired with Louie. The money means little or nothing, thanks to inflation, whatever."

"'Inflation,'" Flynn mused.

Flynn and Randy stood up when Elsbeth entered the living room.

So did Dr. Francine Huong.

"Are you Elsbeth Flynn?" Francine asked.

"I have that pleasure," Elsbeth answered.

"Francine Huong. I'm sorry to burst in on you this way. I met your husband yesterday. I'm afraid I'm taking advantage of a short acquaintance with your husband as an opportunity to meet you."

With a straight face, Elsbeth said, "It's a great thrill meeting me. The man in the produce department says so every time I approach the banana stand."

They all sat.

Elsbeth sat on the edge of her chair. She crossed her ankles. She folded her hands in her lap.

Flynn wondered what his wife was playing at.

Francine took one of Elsbeth's slim volumes from her handbag. "I brought only one of your volumes. My favorite. Hoping you'd sign it for me?"

"Oh, no." Elsbeth raised her nose. "I never sign my books. For that, you'll have to get in touch with my vice president in charge of public relations. If you write him, in San Francisco, maybe he'd sign it for you. My secretary will get you his address."

Francine's cheekbones colored. "Oh, I'm sorry."

Flynn said. "And you have to send him a check for $750.00, plus postage."

Francine looked slapped. "I didn't understand."

"Baseball players get paid for their autographs now," Elsbeth said. "Since when are baseball players more important than poets?"

Francine was putting the book back in her handbag.

Looking at each other, Mr. and Mrs. Flynn laughed. Hard.

Randy did not crack a smile.

Elsbeth held out her hand to Francine. "We're playing a joke on you, Dr. Huong!"

Flynn said, "Satire can be cruel."

"I'll be delighted to sign your book for you. Wait until I get a pin to take blood from my arm."

"Oh. I see." Francine handed Elsbeth the book and her pen. "Two boys who look alike—except one boy's eyes are a lot bigger than the other's—" She laughed. "I love you all!"

"You haven't met Winny yet. He wants to put a television on top of my piano." While signing the book, Elsbeth asked, "You got the leg of lamb, Frannie?"

"Yes."

"Spaghetti tonight."

"Meatloaf, last night," Randy seemed to explain to Francine.

Elsbeth scowled at her son. "So what's wrong with lamb on Sunday?"

"Your word use fascinates me," Francine said to Elsbeth. "I don't write. Well, academic things, of course. But the publishers these days so restrict the words we use, how we use them. Sometimes I think I'm writing a manual on how to build a box."

Elsbeth shook her head sadly.

"I've stuck some papers in the book to mark a few passages . . . Would you mind reading them to me? Just a few verses. So maybe I can hear how it sounds to you."

"Certainly."

Flynn slapped his son on his knee. "Well!" he huffed. "I know when I'm not wanted!"

No one seemed to notice his leaving the room.

Randy did not leave with him. He remained sitting, as if struck by a boulder.

"Thank God," Flynn said to himself, climbing the staircase. "If your typical teenaged American boy knew he was attending a meeting between a Harvard professor and a poet, surely he'd run right out and mug an old lady in the street, just to keep up his pride!"

FOURTEEN

In her pajamas, Jenny crawled into the reading light on her father's lap.

"What are you reading?" she asked.

"*Billy.* By Albert French."

She took the book he was within a few pages of finishing. She looked at the picture of the ten-year-old boy on the front cover. "He looks poor. What's it about? Racism?"

"At the moment, I think it's about capital punishment."

"Oh." Losing track of the book in her hands, she turned more on her side in his lap.

She smelled of soap from her bath.

"Tell me," Flynn said. "Has Billy yet told you who pinned his ear to the tree, and why?"

"No."

"Not even whispered it to you?"

"No."

"Do you think he'll ever tell you?"

"Maybe someday. After we're married."

"Married! Are you going to marry Billy?"

"Someday."

"I thought you were going to marry Mr. I. M. Fletcher."

"That nice man who sent me that beautiful ruby and diamond pin?"

"None other."

She thought a moment. "Maybe I'll just keep him as a sugar daddy."

Amazed she knew such an expression, pretty sure she did not know what it really meant, he laughed. "Ah! That would serve him right, my bit of fluff!"

"Da."

"Yes, Ms. Fluff?"

"That's exactly what I want to talk to you about."

"What?"

"This calling me 'Ms. Fluff' business."

"I've always called you 'Ms. Fluff.'"

"But why?"

"Because you are my bit of fluff."

"I'm not fluff at all."

"To me, aren't you whatever I say you are?"

"I'm me."

"That's right. You're my marvelous Jenny."

"You never call Todd or Randy or Winny 'Fluff.'"

"No. I don't."

"Fluff is . . ."

"What?"

"A dust ball. Something useless. Soft and useless."

"Soft, yes."

"I'm not soft."

"Of course not."

"I'm as . . . hard as the boys."

"Determined, yes."

"Tough."

"Tough, of course."

"I get straight A's in school."

"Yes. You do."

"I swim better than they do."

"Much better."

"I can get every one of them in a half nelson and other wrestling holds and they can't get free. Billy's shown me how."

"Is that so?"

"You love Mother."

"Absolutely."

"You don't call her 'Fluff.'"

"I couldn't."

Jenny blinked slowly. She was half asleep. "Then why me?"

"Ah, you don't understand."

"No."

"If a man is very lucky, you see, there are three women in his life he loves best of all. His mother—"

"You found your mother shot dead on the kitchen floor when you were fourteen. With your father."

"Yes."

"Did you think of your mother as 'fluff'?"

"Oh, no. A mother must give orders which must be obeyed. And with his wife a man experiences many things. Carnal love. Companionship. Responsibility. Anxiety. Childbirth. Hope. Grief. Exhaustion. Respect. In the case of your mother and me, terror, flight . . ."

Jenny blinked again. "Who's the third woman?"

"A man's daughter. Or daughters, if he's fortunate."

"So why must a man think of his daughter as soft? Because he first knew her as a baby?"

"A man doesn't think of his daughter as soft." His arms gave her a little squeeze. "At least this man doesn't think of this daughter as soft."

"You call me 'Fluff.'"

"It's that a man's love for his daughter is soft. It's the softest love that he has." Jenny was thinking. "It's not you that's soft, Jenny. It's my love for you that's soft."

With the speed of a small bird, Jenny raised her head. She kissed his chin.

"Now, then: Will you still permit me to call you 'Fluff'?"

"Oh, yes." Her head was back on his chest. "But not in public."

FIFTEEN

—◆—

"Good morning, Grover. Did you enjoy your quiet day at home yesterday?"

"I didn't have a quiet day at home."

"Not?"

"I spent it with the Lovesons."

Grover had called Flynn's house very early in the morning asking Flynn to pick him up at his home. Then, he said, for reasons of protection, they should drive Professor Loveson to Harvard.

Now, his left wrist in a cast, the blue marks on his face more blue, he sat beside Flynn in the front seat of the unmarked police car.

"You didn't work on the Policepersons' Ball?"

"There are enough people working on that," Grover answered. "I wanted to make sure Professor Loveson was okay."

"I see." Flynn eased the police car politely out into traffic. "You just went over to visit them?"

"I called first. I brought lunch."

"Grover, you surprise me."

"Why?"

"I've never known you to do anything good-hearted before."

"Maybe you don't know me."

"I've always felt I've known you well enough."

"The professor is someone special."

"I see."

"I mean, he thinks about us. People. He's not all the time thinking about oh, money and things, how to screw people. He wants to teach us other things, like who and what and where we are in the universe: that's what he said to me yesterday when we took a walk together, who and what and where I am in the universe. I never thought about all that before. He makes me feel important."

"Egocentric."

"I don't know what that means."

"You took a walk with him?"

"After lunch. I brought them Chinese take-out food for lunch. They were polite about it, but I don't think they liked it much. They had nothing in their refrigerator! Old butter, milk, three eggs. So after lunch I took the professor to a grocery store. I don't think he's ever been in one before. He was amazed at the magazines he saw, you know, all about the moon baby they found in Arizona, and the lady who gave birth to a goat? I taught him about frozen dinners. For supper, I bought them some steak, and potatoes, creamed corn. Boy, they really ate that up! You'd think they hadn't eaten in years."

"You made dinner for them?"

"What's the matter with that?"

"Not a thing. I didn't know you can cook."

"I'm a bachelor, Flynn. I have to eat, don't I?"

"Will wonders never cease? Where was the woman who works for them, Mrs. McElroy, while you did her job for her?"

"He did mention a woman who works for them. He said he gave her the day off because he'd be at home with his wife. Whoever she is, she doesn't do a very good job. That place is not clean. Only old Mrs. Loveson was there. She's as off as the milk in her refrigerator."

"Yes."

"I like her, though. She reminds me of my granny, who brought me and my sister up. By the time we got back from shopping, she had forgotten who I was."

"You left her alone while you went shopping?"

"Had to. The professor couldn't find his keys."

"So Mrs. Loveson let you in, when you returned?"

"Yeah. She doesn't forget who the professor is. Although sometimes she thinks it's forty years ago, or something. Maybe I'll buy her a little television."

"Grover!"

"What? They're a nice old couple. Nobody seems to give a damn for them. Why would anybody try to run over Professor Loveson?"

"Why, indeed."

"He gave me some books to read. I started one last night, when I got home. Just guys hangin' out together, talkin' 'bout things, you know, the way we do sometimes at Hooligan's Bar after work? Well, no, you don't know One of them is named Socrates. You ever read that book?"

Flynn said, "I saw the movie."

———

"Thank you for picking me up, Richard." Professor Louis Loveson got into the backseat of the police car. "Good morning, Inspector Flynn."

That was what the professor said, even though Flynn was driving, had gotten out, rung the professor's apartment bell, waited for him, opened the car door for him.

Driving onto Storrow Drive, Flynn was smiling broadly.

"Did you find your keys, Professor?" Grover asked.

"I did, Richard. Thank you for asking." The professor was carrying a manila envelope. "They were right on my bureau where I usually leave them. I can't guess why I didn't see them yesterday."

Through the rearview mirror, Flynn noticed the expression on the professor's face was unusually dour.

Once on Storrow Drive, the professor kept his eyes on the sun glinting on the surface of Charles River.

"It's hardly my fault that the Scottish were one of the few cultures which even attempted to educate women."

"Sorry?" Flynn was getting used to the way Professor Loveson spoke.

He was a lecturer.

He lectured.

"One has to work from documentary evidence," the professor said. "That is all we have. What is written, in one way or another. What is discoverable from physical evidence, some form of markings, the written word, visual arts, domestic organizations. We cannot just make up history. Goodness me, one of the major things core civilization propagates is the concept of a written language!"

Sitting straight in his seat, Grover had one ear cocked to the backseat.

"My point is," the professor said, "that now that we are developing means of tracing the histories of other cultures, even of other peoples among us, we are doing so. I have spent my life in various parts of the world doing so, encouraging others to do so. My wife and I have made the most horrible human sacrifice in doing so. I have rejected nothing that is valid! Why am I being so criticized for excluding the histories and cultures of other peoples when that is exactly not what I have done?"

Flynn finally said, "I guess you have seen what someone put on the Net about you a few days ago?"

"Yes." The professor lifted the manila envelope from his lap and dropped it back down as if it weighed pounds. "It was delivered to me in manuscript form anonymously this morning. So unfair! You have seen it?"

"Yes."

"You didn't tell me."

"No."

"Why not?"

"I didn't feel you had the need to see it."

"There are times in history, natural disasters, wars, economic conditions, that civilizations have hunkered down and asserted this 'Us Against Them' mentality, suppressed others to preserve themselves either rightly or wrongly.

Tribes do this, societies, governments, churches, other institutions. But intellectuals? Never! Artists? Never! Scientists? Never! Not the true navigators! Without the true navigators we three would not be riding along in this car this morning, reasonably sound in mind, eyes, ears, and teeth, speaking a common language. There is and has been and will be suppression, oppression. But those keepers of tradition, who try to broaden traditional understandings on the basis of careful study of valid evidence, are not the suppressors!"

Simply, Flynn said, "You're being accused of excluding every idea except those that keep you in power."

"I'll give you an example," the professor said. "There have been more tons of sculptures, more reams of music, poetry, other writings, there have been more thousands of religious ideas in history than can possibly be recorded, I daresay, even on the ultimate computer. Only those that continue to exist generation after generation can be said to be satisfying some human need. That's all that is important about them. Not that some graybeard has ordained this good and that bad in some foolish effort to keep himself on the top of some useless heap. One idea is not as good as another, chosen arbitrarily by some board of power mongers. It is the idea itself that must continue to fulfill some human need, for that idea to survive. The idea that expresses and satisfies some human need more profoundly and permanently is better than an idea that is thrown up, momentarily considered, if at all, and then discarded because it satisfies no need. Of course the object or the myth isn't necessarily true. It is the continuing human need for it that is true. This process by which the people in each generation continually elect the ideas they need to survive is the true, eternal democracy! Why isn't that clear? You understand that, don't you, Richard?"

Grover's eyes bulged. He swallowed hard. Finally, he shrugged. "Yeah. Why not?"

Flynn was parking the unmarked Boston Police car in a well-marked Cambridge bus stop.

"Inspector Flynn, have you any idea who has attacked me personally and professionally on the electronic toy in this vile and virulent manner?"

"Yes."

"Will you tell me who?"

"No."

The professor began to let himself out of the backseat. "I still teach a class. I still keep office hours. If these people had the character tradition should have given them they would have attacked me and my work in a less anonymous manner. Don't you agree?"

"Yes," Flynn said.

Before getting out of the car, Grover whispered to Flynn, "What's in the envelope?"

"Cartoons."

"Of the professor?"

"Yes."

Rage filled Grover's face. "Someone drew cartoons of the professor?"

"That's right."

"I'll pull the head off the rat who did that!"

"Fractionalization, Inspector Flynn," the professor said.

They were walking through Harvard Yard to the professor's office.

In front of them walked Grover in sunglasses, watching the hands of everyone who approached them. As he walked along he looked behind every tree. Apparently, he was even scanning the roofs of the surrounding buildings for snipers.

"'Fractionalization.'" Flynn knew he need encourage the professor no further for him to continue his thought.

"You were at the cocktail party at Dean Wincomb's house."

"Yes."

"Didn't you notice the people there? Black people keeping to themselves, those of Asian derivation in a separate huddle, women making their own little exclusive group, people of one generation not talking to people of another generation?"

"It was pretty obvious."

"Not too many years ago I could have brought those people together. Given them a sense of commonality. Of the human race, the human experience, as a whole. You know, we're-all-in-the-same-boat-together sort of thing."

Flynn said, "Eric Hoffer. I'm sure you've read him." Professor Loveson stared at him. "In order to bring people together you must provide them with a common enemy."

Staring sideways at Flynn, Loveson tripped on the edge of the sidewalk.

Grover whipped around.

Flynn grabbed Loveson's elbow and steadied him. "That's all right, Grover."

Loveson said, "I think you are one very strange cop, Inspector Flynn. How do you explain yourself?"

Flynn chuckled. "I'm lying doggo. Lacking an invasion from Mars, you might consider doing the same."

———

Loveson unlocked the door to his office and pushed it open.

Immediately, he gasped.

"What's wrong?" Grover stepped in front of him and entered the room first.

Flynn entered second.

Loveson remained standing in the doorway. He looked around. "This," he said.

The floor was shin-high with torn paper.

Every book and magazine from the shelves had been taken down and ripped apart. Their spines looked like the wings of so many dead birds. Drawers of the filing cabinets and desk had been turned out. Manuscript pages had been torn lengthwise and then across and apparently thrown to scatter them widely. Pictures, award citations from the walls had been smashed against a corner of the desk, and then shredded.

Two Harvard chairs were tipped over in the mess.

"This," Loveson said.

"Who has a key to this office?" Flynn asked.

"Flynn." Grover was looking at Loveson.

Still in the doorway, Loveson's face had grayed. Sweat gleamed on his forehead. His right hand rubbed his chest.

"This," Loveson said, "will kill me."

Somehow getting his feet through the mess on the floor

and despite his left wrist being in a cast, Grover caught
Loveson as he collapsed. Turning him over, he eased him
gently to the floor.

"You work on him," Flynn said. "I'll find a working
phone."

SIXTEEN

"How do you feel now?" Flynn stood by Loveson's bed at Mt. Auburn Hospital.

The professor seemed held together by tubes. He was controlling his own oxygen mask.

"Ah, Richard," Loveson said. "You're still here."

Grover stood behind Flynn.

"Professor," Flynn asked, "how can I get in touch with your daughter?"

"I don't have a daughter."

Out of the corner of his eye, Flynn saw Grover take Loveson's hand in his.

"Sir," Flynn said. "You once mentioned having a daughter to me. When I was saying something about my daughter, Jenny—"

"I don't have a daughter."

"All right." Flynn took a step back. "I'll look in on Mrs. Loveson for you."

"Before you go, Flynn . . ." Loveson spoke through a dry mouth. "Please turn off the television."

While Flynn fumbled around trying to find out how to turn off the television, Loveson continued: "My younger colleagues take nonlinear thought as an intellectual posture. What they don't realize is that the biggest intellectual influence upon their lives has been the television, which is not capable of being linear for three minutes together. No wonder they eschew linear thought. They are incapable of it."

Flynn finally found the switch. The television screen went blank.

Loveson said, "I'm afraid these generations will end up as crazy as Ezra Pound."

With a nod of his head, Flynn indicated Grover should follow him out of the room.

In the corridor, Grover shook his head. "He keeps on saying what he wants to say, no matter what. Isn't he wonderful?"

"Extraordinary."

"Will it be all right with you if I stay with him for a while?"

"All right," Flynn said. "But as people arrive to see him, do not identify yourself as a police officer. Say you're just a friend."

Grover said, "I am just a friend."

Grover's eyes were wet.

In the hospital lobby, Flynn met Dean Wincomb entering.

"How is he?" the dean asked.

"Stable. He's had a heart attack."

"Inspector, I've had a phone call."

"Yes?"

"I don't know how else to do this. Could you come to my office? Would two o'clock be convenient for you?"

"Yes."

The dean said, "I think we'll have something interesting to tell you."

Flynn let himself back into Professor Loveson's office.

After the paramedics lifted Loveson out of the office on a gurney, Flynn had found Loveson's keys in the rubble on the floor. He had locked the door.

Nothing appeared to have been disturbed in the trashed room.

Flynn thought he had seen some papers of particular interest to him among the thousands of pieces of paper on the floor. They stood out because of the colors on them.

As he picked out these pieces of paper on the floor, he noticed they were the only papers which had not been torn.

U R GOING TO DIE

Another: WHY DON'T YOU KILL YOURSELF?

Another: JUST DIE

DIE OR WE'LL KILL U

U R A EVIL MAN

There were dozens of such notes.

The letters and some whole words had been cut out from magazines, and glued onto sheets of paper torn from cheap ruled ring notebooks.

U R GOING TO DIE A HORRIBLE DEATH

U DIE WITHIN MONTH

U DIE IN TWO WEEKS

U DIE IN ONE WEEK

Flynn collected all such notes he could find. He tried to handle them by only their upper-left edges. He hoped forensics would be able to lift fingerprints from them.

As he did so, he postulated that, seeing none of these pieces of papers was torn, whoever had trashed Professor Loveson's office was probably the same person who had written them.

"Ah, vanity, vanity," Flynn said. "Isn't it wonderful, what it will do to you?"

———

"Come in, Inspector Flynn." Dean Wincomb rose from behind his desk. "Please close the door."

Assistant Professor Don Carver did not rise from his chair in front of the desk. He twisted his neck to look at Flynn as if to read his face.

"Ah, Carver!" Flynn looked down at him. "So you're ready to confess."

"I suspect my young colleague is afraid of being charged with manslaughter," Wincomb muttered. "Please sit down, Inspector."

"I'll stand." Flynn held the manila envelope he had bought at the Harvard Coop under his arm. In it were the threatening notes.

Sitting behind his desk, Dean Wincomb sighed. "You called this meeting, Don. The floor is yours."

"Yes. Well." Carver hitched himself higher in his chair. "I

was in the building when they took old Loveson out this morning."

"You're referring to Professor Louis Loveson?" Flynn asked.

Carver amended himself. "Professor Loveson. He had a heart attack, did he?"

"Yes."

"Will he be all right?"

"Who knows?" said Wincomb.

Flynn said, "His office has been trashed. His books, files, manuscripts. If he's not dead, the center of his world is."

Carver studied his hands twisting in his lap. "I want you to know I didn't do it."

"Do what?" asked Flynn.

"I did not trash his office."

"Let's start with what you did do," said Flynn.

"I did put that stuff on the Net about him, his work, earlier this week."

"'Stuff'!" Flynn said. "What a literary term, Assistant Professor! Could you try for a more academic description of that manuscript?"

Carver tilted his head to the side. "Stupid stuff. A critique. I was trying to expose—well, maybe—the single-mindedness of Loveson's work."

"You did it anonymously," Dean Wincomb said. "It was an anonymous, vicious attack."

"Well, yes. The Net provides one with that kind of freedom."

"With the possibility of complete irresponsibility," Wincomb said.

"'The electronic toy.'" Flynn looked at the ceiling, which was not much above his head. "The great poison pen."

"It's all right," Carver insisted. "What is written on the Net is as true as anything else."

"Is it?" With both hands, Wincomb was fiddling with a pen on his desk. "I don't wonder you may think all academic discipline has been abandoned."

"I have my First Amendment rights!"

"You have abrogated academic responsibilities," said Wincomb. "Let alone human decency."

"You have the right," Flynn said, "to stand on a lemon crate on the commons and say anything you wish. And those who disagree with you have the right to boo you. You have the right to publish your thoughts—signed. You do not have the right to assault people anonymously."

"I did not trash his office."

Flynn asked, "Have you been making anonymous, threatening phone calls to Professor Loveson?"

There was a slight smile from Carver. "I'm not the only one. A group of us . . . We'd get conversing on the Net regarding the works of Louie Loveson . . . making fun of them. Of him. Like, you know, his spending his life running around in only the center of the maze. We'd think of some funny way of insulting his work, him." He looked up at Flynn. "'Threatening'? No. We never actually threatened him. Not with bodily harm. Nothing like that."

"Please do not touch these." Flynn permitted gravity to slide the threatening notes onto Wincomb's desk. "If your fingerprints are already on them, we'll find out soon enough."

The men on both sides of the desk leaned forward to look at the notes.

Wincomb shook his head. "Disgusting."

"Did you or your group of colleagues send these missives to Professor Louis Loveson?"

Carver looked frankly at Flynn. "No. Absolutely not. These aren't funny."

"No," Flynn said. "They're not."

Carver said, "Of course, I can't swear to what other people do, have done. I can't believe anyone I know would do a stupid thing like that. They're childish!"

By tapping the edges of the papers, Flynn slid them back into the envelope. "You and I may have different ideas as to what is childish," Flynn said. "I've visited your home."

Wincomb sat up. In a somber voice he advised Carver, "Your teaching contract will not be renewed."

Carver looked shocked.

"I believe this is reason for immediate dismissal," Flynn said.

Carver looked more shocked at Flynn.

"You're on suspension as of now," Wincomb said.

Mouth open, Carver's head swiveled back and forth between Wincomb and Flynn like a tennis ball being hit by both sides.

"I believe he should be made an example of," Flynn said.

"We do not wish to make a public issue of this, Inspector Flynn."

Flynn remembered the President's words: "I really don't want a written record of this, if you understand me. Unless, of course, something happens and it is unavoidable."

Fists on his chair arms, eyes blazing, Carver said to Wincomb, "Well, maybe I'll make an issue of this! I have my rights!"

"Fine." Wincomb smiled. "Develop that sort of a reputation for yourself. Maybe someday you'll be able to get a job teaching in a boys' reformatory."

"If you do make an issue of it, as you say," Flynn said, "I'm afraid you'll embarrass me. I'll have to leave it up to the attorney general's office whether criminal charges should be filed against you."

Taut with anger, Carver went to the door. He slammed it open.

Heading down the corridor, he shouted, "I did not trash Loveson's office!"

Slouched behind his desk, Dean Wincomb asked Flynn, "Who did? Who wrote those notes?"

Flynn said, "Damned if I know."

Even though he had the keys, Flynn rang the doorbell to the Lovesons' apartment.

He rang it again.

And again.

The door jerked open as much as its chain permitted.

"Mrs. McElroy, is it? Inspector Flynn. Boston Police. We met the other day."

"What you want now?"

"To come in, please."

She considered it.

Finally she opened the door. "The professor no is here."

"I know that. I need your help on something. How is Mrs. Loveson today?"

The woman shrugged fat shoulders. "Still crazy."

The woman wore necklaces from which hung silver ornaments. Some were of pyramids. Some of camels.

A twisted silver ring on her finger was of a snake.

"I see. That's why I need your help. What's your first name?"

Warily, the woman answered, "Enid."

"Ah, yes." They were still standing in the foyer. "May we sit down, Enid?"

The powder and rouge on her face did not conceal to Flynn the heavy, lifetime exposure to the sun her skin had suffered.

She shrugged, turned and led him into the living room.

Enid wore a long, black dress over her big frame. On it, in red, were Aramaic letters. The letters were arranged meaninglessly.

Callie Loveson's eyes lit up when she saw Flynn. "Ah, we have a visitor! How nice!"

Enid said, "She's as well as can be expected."

"How do, Mrs. Loveson." Flynn extended his hand to her. The seated obese woman took it gracefully. "My name is Flynn."

"Yes," she said. "Mary, do get us a nice tea."

Enid sat in her recliner.

Over heavy socks Enid wore very old sandals.

Flynn sat on the divan. "How long have you been working for the Lovesons, Enid?"

"Tree monts."

"I see. It must be tiresome. This small apartment. No television."

"It all right. Not much to do."

Smiling in a friendly manner, Flynn asked Callie Loveson, "What did you two have for lunch today?"

Callie frowned in thought. Then beamed. "We had a game hen! And wild rice. It was excellent, wasn't it, E — nid. The waiter was so kind!"

"I brought a can of chicken soup," Enid said. "She don't know no diff'runce."

"Enid—" Flynn looked at her heavily made-up face for as long as he could bear. "We need to be in touch with the Loveson's daughter."

"Daughter? What daughter?"

"Does she live locally?"

"No daughter." Her hands grabbed up the sides of her skirt and put them in her lap. "No daughter."

"But there is a daughter. Professor Loveson mentioned her to me once . . ."

"No daughter!" Enid sat forward in her recliner.

Flynn looked toward the kitchen counter. "Do the Lovesons have some sort of a telephone-address book? They must have."

"No. Calls coming in only. Professor he never use telephone."

"Instrument of the devil, is it?" Flynn went to the kitchen area. Indeed there was a green address book near the phone.

There was no listing under Loveson.

How could he ever identify a daughter if he did not know her married name?

The book was very old. Flicking through it he saw nothing that looked like a recent entry. Recent in years.

"Do you happen to know her first name, Enid? Ever hear them mention their daughter by name?"

The woman was sitting sideways on the edge of her recliner.

Looking at Enid from the kitchen area, Flynn asked, "When was the last time you were in Egypt?"

"Egypt." She rose quickly. "Never been in Egypt. I go now." She took her coat from a hall closet. "Professor Loveson be here soon. You stay."

"But, Enid— It's just after four o'clock."

She struggled into her coat. It was more of a useless vest. It was nothing anyone would wear in the New England climate for warmth.

"You can't go," Flynn said. "I must tell you—make arrangements—"

Enid McElroy was out the door.

Instantly, Flynn heard the elevator door close.

"Um," he said.

Flynn went to the living-room window at the front of the apartment. He wanted to see if he had much hope of catching up with Mrs. Enid McElroy.

Variously parked in the street were three small blue cars.

Enid McElroy was already getting into one.

Her huge eyes on Flynn when he turned, Callie Loveson said, "It's very difficult to get good servants these days, isn't it?"

SEVENTEEN

"Are you the new doctor?" Callie Loveson asked Flynn.

He sat on the edge of the recliner abandoned by Enid McElroy.

"Do you wish to think so?" Flynn asked, appropriately enough.

"Oh, yes. You're very nice."

"Thank you."

"I think it very odd, don't you? That ever since Louie had his head broken all you doctors have been concerned about is what's going on in my head."

"Louie had his head broken?"

"I don't mind. Am I going back to the hospital now? I haven't been feeling too well lately. Who was that woman who just left? Rather a pig, isn't she. Traditionally, religions have thought ill of the pig, until Christianity came to the South." She rolled her tongue around her lips. "Barbecue."

"Are you nervous with me?" Flynn asked.

"Something's happened to Louie."

"What?"

"He's in the hospital, isn't he?"

"Yes."

"He got his head broken. They pushed him down. Stamped his head into the road. They broke his head and they've been treating me for a broken head ever since. Tell me the sense of that!"

"When was that? When was Louie's head broken?"

Callie Loveson looked alarmed. "This morning? You said he's in the hospital now."

"Yes."

"Will he be all right? I doubt it. Of course I'm nervous. What do you think?"

"Where did this happen? Where did Louie get his head broken?"

"Big city. By the sea. New York? No. I remember now. Alexandria, Virginia. That's a nice place."

"Who stamped on Louie's head? Who broke his head?"

"Well, you know the answer to that! You were probably there! You seem to know a lot! The men who took the girl from Louie. At least, that's what the man from the embassy said. I really don't like him much. Will you please ask him to stop coming to see me?"

"He won't come see you anymore."

"That's nice. You're very kind."

"What girl?"

"She's the secretary for the man from the embassy. I don't like her, either. She keeps looking at me as if I'm crazy, or something. I keep testing her out, you see. I say things like, 'The river is full of chocolate pudding,' and she says, 'Yes, all right.' Crazy! She's the crazy one. I don't need to see her anymore, either."

"All right. You won't. Was she with Louie when his head was broken?"

"They pushed him right down. Against the wall. Well, you told me that. Then they stamped on his head."

"What happened to the girl?"

"Well, that's it, isn't it?"

"That's what?"

"There is no girl. There never was, you see. That is what one had better think."

"What happened to the girl?"

"The girl getting the tea? I think she just left. I told her you like cream puffs. I remember that about you. I told her to make cream puffs especially for you."

"Thank you."

Shrewdly, Callie Loveson looked at Flynn. "She's probably gone to the river to get the chocolate pudding for the cream puffs."

"There is no chocolate pudding in the river," Flynn said.

Callie laughed. "You're a sane one!"

"Well . . ."

"What day is this?"

"Thursday."

"Yes. I've been out of the hospital three months now. And three days." She looked perplexed at the piles of magazines around her chair. "But why am I the one who goes to the hospital when it was Louie who had his head broken? We were in New York for a long time, you see. Well, I went to see him in the hospital there. That man from the embassy took me. Then they kept me in the hospital! I suppose it was cheaper than the hotel. Do you think that's why they kept me in the hospital?"

"Possibly."

"Because I didn't see that much of Louie in the hospital. Then I got sick. The hospital began to sway back and forth, up and down. My stomach got sick. My head ached. Louie was with me then. Did you know New York floats?"

"Certainly. New York floats everything."

"After a while, the hospital settled down. All that motion stopped. Then they planted trees outside the hospital. Put hills around there. That was nice. Except for Mrs. Roberts. She wasn't nice. Your name is Winthrop, isn't it?"

"I live in Winthrop."

"I remember. I've been back to that hospital many times. It's wonderful how they can change the shape of the hills outside the windows these days, isn't it?"

While listening, Flynn was trying to figure out what to do with Mrs. Loveson. The woman who was supposed to take care of her had run out. He had no idea how to reach her. He wasn't sure he would if he could. At least not to return to take care of Mrs. Loveson. In the hospital, Professor Loveson assumed his wife was being taken care of.

Flynn wondered if Elsbeth, through her charities, knew of someone who could come and stay with Mrs. Loveson.

It surely wasn't Elsbeth's problem.

He supposed he would have to call an agency called Human Services or something. Would Cocky know how to be in touch with the right agency? What to tell them? Of course.

Flynn thought he probably would have to wait hours before someone from some agency showed up to say what should be done with Mrs. Loveson.

"Did you have a nice tea?" Callie asked him.

"Oh, yes. Thank you. The éclairs were excellent."

"It's better not to think of things like that," Callie said.

"Of course not."

"I mean, like what happens to girls."

"That's right."

"What happens, happens, I always say. I mean, people sometimes do get their heads broken."

"Yes."

"They can still become Harvard professors."

Flynn said, "I think it helps."

"The doorbell is about to ring," Callie said.

"Is it?"

The doorbell rang.

"It always clicks like that first."

"I see." Flynn's perfect ears had not heard a click. "Who is at the door?" Flynn asked her.

She frowned. "It's not Louie. He's in the hospital."

In the front hall, Flynn pushed the button of the door intercom. "Who is it?"

Callie said, "Richard."

"Flynn?"

"Ah, Grover. It's you, is it?"

"Ring the buzzer."

"Ah, yes. Happily."

He did so. Opened the apartment's front door. Heard the elevator rise the three stories.

Grover came out of the elevator with a big brown paper bag cradled in his right arm.

Flynn stood back to let him enter. "Grover, I'm glad to

see you! I never thought I'd hear myself saying that. Let me take the bag."

"I brought food for Mrs. Loveson."

"How kind."

"How is she? Did you tell her . . . ?"

"She seems to know Loveson's in the hospital. Thought I'd leave it at that."

Flynn placed the bag on the kitchen table.

"Hi, Mrs. Loveson!" Grover said cheerily.

"How good to see you!" Her eyes beamed.

"Where's the woman?" Grover asked. "The one who's supposed to be taking care of Mrs. Loveson?"

"She fled almost the moment I arrived. Before I had a chance to tell her we have a problem."

"No problem," Grover said.

"We haven't a problem?"

"No. I'll stay with Mrs. Loveson tonight."

"Grover, you can't!"

"I'll sleep on the couch."

"Grover, you can't take care of an unwell old woman! Feed her. Put her to bed."

"Of course I can. My sister and I took care of my old Granny more than five years, when she was this way. Mostly I did. My sister did better at school than I did."

"And where was your uncle, Captain Walsh, while all this was going on?"

"He visited his mother Sundays. Some Sundays."

"I think I'm beginning to understand."

"Understand what?"

"Lots of things." While Grover took off his coat, Flynn

was taking bread, eggs, bacon, pork chops, baked beans, chocolate éclairs out of the bag. "Nothing is ever absolutely senseless, is it? If you follow it far enough."

Grover said, "I discovered last night I had to wash the pots and pans before I cooked in them. The glasses, dishes, knives, and forks . . ."

"Grover, why don't we call the Department of Human Services, or whatever it's called. Then maybe you'd have the goodness to wait here for them to come do whatever they do?"

"No. I want to do this. I'll stay with her. Take care of her. I owe Professor Loveson this much."

"Grover, you've known the man only a few days!"

"That's all right. Flynn, you're always sayin' things I don't understand."

"So you say."

"The professor makes sure I understand what he says."

"He's kind . . . ?"

Grover almost said the obvious. Instead he said, "Why don't you just go get your appendix out? It must have grown back again by now."

Flynn grinned. "I'm so pleased by you, I might just do that. Make a present of this one to you."

"I got some cream puffs." Grover put them in the refrigerator. "Do you think Mrs. Loveson likes cream puffs?"

"I'm certain of it. Oh, here are Professor Loveson's keys." Flynn was putting on his coat. "Just don't tell her you got the chocolate pudding from the river. She'll think you're crazy."

In various places in the Flynn home that night after dinner three violins were practicing three different sections of a Mozart piece simultaneously. They were being practiced for the Flynn family's Sunday afternoon living-room musicale.

Jet airplanes flew over the roof as they took off from and landed at Logan International Airport just across the harbor.

Flynn found his wife working on a computer in the den.

"Will you be free to take a walk?"

"Lovely idea," she said. "The sweet music of the Flynn household getting to you? Me, too. Let me just finish logging this verse. There! Here. Come read it."

She scrolled all three verses onto the screen.

"This poem has taken me eleven months. Sometimes having a child is quicker."

Leaning over her, he read the poem.

"Do you like it?" she asked.

He read it again. "Very much. I shall enjoy reading that piece for the rest of my life."

"Thank you," she said. "Would you like to see a note Winny left for me? You know my poem about how an alcoholic sees the world, in which I use every word there is for the color red?"

"Sure."

"This is the note Winny left me."

She scrolled up.

There appeared on the screen:

Mama,
*   As you know I like your poem WELL . . . RED very*

much. But I'd see all those reds better if once you used
the word "green."

Winny

"Isn't that wonderful?" Elsbeth asked. "And you know what? He's right! Nine years old and he's right!"

She turned off the computer.

———

As she marched beside Flynn along the dark sidewalk, beneath Elsbeth's good tweed skirt her sensible brown shoes kicked up dead leaves rhythmically.

Elsbeth grasped Flynn's point regarding Lieutenant Detective John Kurt before he made it.

"That bears further looking into," she said.

"Yes."

"One man using his uniform and gun only to exercise his prejudices is like the little match that can set the world afire. Prejudice is the original sin, and it will destroy the world yet."

"Cocky tells me Kurt seems to be the center of a growing pool of young admirers, among the police."

Elsbeth told Flynn that her new publisher suggested illustrating her next book of poetry. "'If the images I make in your head aren't better than what an artist can do with pen and ink, then don't publish me,' I told him."

"The image is the illustration, isn't it?" Flynn asked.

He then brought Elsbeth up to date on the affair Loveson.

He flashed his pocket light along the cemetery wall to find the break in it. There was no moon this night.

"This is where Jenny brought me Sunday night. Over the wall just here."

Elsbeth climbed over the cemetery wall. "I don't suppose we're supposed to be in the cemetery after dark."

Flynn followed her over the wall. "I don't think many want to be."

"Think of all the places, Franny, people haven't wanted you and me."

"Everywhere."

"Do we go uphill?"

"Yes."

She took his hand. "We've made a difference, you and I."

"One way and another," he said.

Trudging up the cemetery hillside slippery with dead leaves, she said, "But how many times do I have to remind you, Franny, you think too much. You're too philosophical. You want to see into things too deeply."

"What are you talking about now?"

"This Loveson business. You're doing it again. You're trying to understand all this as some beginning-of-the-century academic jostling for position. You just said you think it's existential nihilism in a new form."

"And what should I be thinking? I must understand the people involved, what concerns them, what they're thinking."

"What do I always tell you? At the bottom of every difficulty, criminal or not: always a little schnook with a grievance."

At the top of the hill, she asked, "So where's the children's trysting place?"

"Over here." Flynn moved to his left. "This way."

"You remember our place in the olive orchard, Franny, in that little town outside Basra?"

"We were older."

"They would have killed us."

"That was part of the fun. Wasn't it?" He shined his light on the thick oak. "That's where the boy lover got his ear nailed to the tree."

"Poor Billy."

"Louie Loveson suggested whoever nailed Billy to the tree thought Billy was 'unmanly.' Had done something 'unmanly.' What's considered 'unmanly' these days?"

"Not wearing an earring high up in the ear apparently."

"Look at that!" Flynn's light had passed over a tombstone. "Capriano!" He ran his light around other tombstones surrounding them. "Capriano, Capriano! We're in the Capriano family plot! I knew I had seen that name in some odd place recently. I'll be . . . ! I guess when I was here Sunday I didn't know Billy's last name was Capriano."

He went to the most recent grave. "This does have something to do with his family."

Crouching before the most recent tombstone, Flynn read TERESA CAPRIANO, her date of birth, her date of death just five years past.

On the same tombstone was inscribed ANTONIO CAPRIANO. His date of birth was five years earlier than his wife's. There was no date of death.

Flynn said, "Billy's grandfather is still alive."

"Sure," Elsbeth said. "Mr. Anthony. A fine old gentleman. Seldom comes to the store anymore. He's nearly eighty."

"Yes, he is," Flynn said.

"You never met Mr. Anthony?"

"I guess not. But I was reasonably certain neither Billy's father nor uncle nailed Billy's ear to the tree."

"You think Mr. Anthony did?"

"I sure do." Flynn stood up. "But I still don't know why."

EIGHTEEN

Sitting at the chess table in the alcove near the fireplace in his office on Craigie Lane Friday morning, Flynn continued to stare at the figures on the chessboard after he had moved his knight.

Cocky brought the two cups of herb tea into the office on a tray held in his right hand.

Glancing at the board, Cocky said, "I thought you'd do that."

"You've given me damn-all choice."

"You had a choice," Cocky said. "You missed it."

"You meant for me to sacrifice something, didn't you?"

Cocky nestled at his side of the board. "I always play to what isn't characteristic of you, Flynn."

He moved his king.

"No!" Flynn said. "You're not doing that!"

"Done it."

"Ah!" Flynn moved a rook.

Cocky moved his king again.

Flynn said, "Oh."

Dragging his left foot a little behind him, Cocky went to answer the phone on Flynn's desk.

"It's Grover," Cocky said. "He says he needs to talk to you."

"Right." Standing at the desk, Flynn said, "Good morning, Sergeant. Did you get any sleep on that couch?"

"Enough. Mrs. Loveson's very peaceful, really."

"In a way, it must be nice."

"Look, Flynn, that woman, what's her name—?"

"Mrs. McElroy."

"—hasn't shown up."

"That doesn't surprise me. Time to call Human Services, Grover, old lad."

"I think I'll try to clean this place up a little."

"Grover, no matter how alarming, I mean, charming is your affection for the Lovesons, the City of Boston is paying neither you nor me to play at baby-sitting."

"Maybe Mrs. McElroy will show up. Why wouldn't she? I don't even know if she has a key."

"She must have."

"You don't know that. Are you going to see Professor Loveson?"

"Yes, I'll visit him in the hospital this morning. I think I have some questions for him. Keep in touch, Grover."

"My name is Richard."

"There's nothing wrong with my having an affectionate name for you, is there?"

Flynn hung up before Grover could answer.

Cocky had been spreading papers around Flynn's desk to display them.

"What's all this about?" Flynn studied the dozens of head shots and short biographies glued to the papers.

"These," Cocky announced slowly, "are all the people Lieutenant Detective John Kurt has convicted in the last eighteen months."

"My, my," said Flynn. "Almost all black."

"One Asian American." Cocky pointed to the picture of a man with a goatee. "Read the names of the four white people."

"Ginsberg, Knowlton, Epstein, Jacobs."

"Three Jews, wouldn't you say?"

"And Knowlton?"

"Read what he was convicted of."

"Solicitation."

"Of a male police officer."

"Homosexual."

"Statistically," Cocky said, "this is highly improbable, if not impossible."

"Does Lieutenant Kurt work in a mainly black district?"

"Distinctly not."

"Then it can be assumed that Lieutenant Kurt, while going out of his way to charge minorities with crimes, is also, most likely, avoiding arresting possible white miscreants."

"He seems to be running a one-man campaign to bring every black, Jew, or sexually other-directed person up on charges. Besides that, Flynn, there appears to be a running gag among his friends that Kurt is absolutely brazen at planting evidence on people he doesn't like. Look at how many weapons charges there are here. Way above a likely average. One of the jokes is that Kurt keeps introducing the same gun as evidence in case after case. Also that he plants drugs on people, as well as stolen property. A big joke is his charging a black paraplegic with the theft of a motorcycle."

"And no one has put this together before . . . ?"

"Why would anybody? Kurt is considered a great success."

"What you're saying, Cocky, is that all these cases will have to be reviewed. As if the courts haven't enough to do!"

The telephone rang.

Flynn answered, saying, "Thank you for calling the Boston Police Department. How may we help you this fine day?"

The right side of Cocky's lips smiled.

There was a momentary silence on the other end of the line. "Flynn?"

"Grover!"

"I'm just trying to straighten out the Lovesons' apartment. There are all these magazines on the floor of the living room, near Mrs. Loveson's chair."

"I've noticed them underfoot."

"When I picked them up to throw them away I realized somebody has been at them with a scissors."

"What do you mean?"

"Inside. Individual letters. Whole words have been cut out of the magazines. Perhaps it's some game Mrs. Loveson plays. You know, preschool activity, or something. Some kind of therapy. Do you think so? If it's some kind of therapy for her, I shouldn't throw these magazines away."

"My, my," Flynn said.

"I can't get Mrs. Loveson to say anything about them. This morning she keeps going on about how to cook a goose."

"Absolutely, Grover, do not throw those magazines away. Not on your life. Don't even touch them or rearrange their order."

"So I'm right. This is some kind of therapy for her?"

"Have you heard from Mrs. McElroy yet?"

"No."

"Keep those magazines," Flynn said. "I want to see them."

Flynn sat at his desk and thought a moment.

He looked at Cocky. "I'm glad to see you have put your insignias back on your uniform."

"I'm fully reinstated."

"Yes, you are. I'm rather hoping you'll accompany me to the Policepersons' Ball this evening."

"I hope not," said Cocky. "I don't dance as well as I used to, you know."

"Who does? Tonight, I'll need you as a witness while I may be committing a crime. I expect to break and enter."

"Okay."

"In fact, you can wait in the car, while I stop in on the ball, if you'd prefer. It's a little later on in the evening that I'll need you."

"Establishing an alibi for yourself, are you?"

"That may be, depending on how things work out. More to the point, I hope to establish the whereabouts of someone else, during my commission of the crime."

Flynn put on his overcoat near his office door. "In the

meantime, please see if you can find for me a woman named Enid McElroy. Mrs. McElroy. She's between forty-five and fifty years old, I should guess. She works as housekeeper, baby-sitter for Professor and Mrs. Loveson. And I'm afraid that's all I can tell you about her."

"Will do."

"I'll call you from the hospital."

———

"Thank you for calling the Boston Police Department," Cocky said into the phone. "How may we help you this fine day?"

At the pay phone just off the lobby of Mt. Auburn Hospital, Flynn laughed.

"I knew it was you," Cocky said.

"Anything on Enid McElroy?"

"Yes. The only Enid McElroy within a hundred miles of Boston is an eleven-year-old girl in Concord, New Hampshire. She has leukemia."

"That's the only one?"

"The only one I can find."

"No driver's license, car registration, credit cards, bank accounts, social security, telephone?"

"None of the above."

"I know our Enid M. drives a car."

"Not one registered to her in Massachusetts, New Hampshire, Vermont, Maine, or Rhode Island. And not with a driver's license granted by any of those states."

"How very interesting."

"I would say your Mrs. McElroy doesn't exist, Frank."

"Indications are very strong, old man, that indeed she does not. Many thanks."

"Anytime you want me not to find someone, Inspector, don't hesitate to call."

———

"I'm glad to see you looking so much better this morning." Flynn drew a chair up to Loveson's bedside. "Richard stayed overnight with Mrs. Loveson."

"I know. He called me last night, so I shouldn't worry."

"How do you actually feel?"

Loveson stared at the blank television screen. "All I can see in my mind's eye is my office torn apart. All those books and manuscripts destroyed. I wouldn't have slept a wink last night, if they hadn't given me pills."

"I'm sorry."

"Without all those papers, I just can't go on."

"You're still Dr. Louis Loveson."

"Am I? Is a plumber still a plumber without his wrench? I've been forced into retirement. Finally."

"I need to talk to you." Flynn watched Loveson's face. "You have a daughter."

Loveson said nothing.

"Let me see if I have this right. When she was a little girl you and Mrs. Loveson took your daughter on one of your research trips, to Alexandria, Egypt. One day you took your daughter with you when you left the hotel. You left your wife at the hotel. In the street, you were attacked by men. They took your daughter from you. Wrested her from you, in fact. They threw you against a wall. While you were lying in the road, they kicked you, possibly stomped on your head. They fractured your skull."

Loveson asked, "How do you know this?"

"Mrs. Loveson told me."

"How is that possible?"

Flynn said, "I listen."

Then Flynn asked, "What was your daughter's name?"

"Clara. She was twelve years old."

"You never saw her again?"

"I assumed she was forced into some form of slavery. I did the best I could. I worked, or tried to work, through the American Embassy with the Egyptian police, even Interpol. I did the best I could, considering I was immobile with a fractured skull. In all the time I was in the hospital, the authorities came up with exactly nothing."

"And Mrs. Loveson?"

"Couldn't bear it, of course. The event deranged her. After a few days, the people from the embassy told me they had to hospitalize her, too. She wasn't eating, sleeping, taking care of herself in any way, even her bodily functions. She had had a complete mental breakdown. By the time I was ready to be released from the hospital, the only thing I could do was arrange to bring Callie back to New York by ship. She's been in and out of mental hospitals ever since. All her memories date from before that incident, before Clara was taken from us." Loveson sipped water through a glass straw. "Callie denies we ever had a daughter, that there ever was a Clara. In a way, she's been happier than I have been, I suppose. All these years I have had to work hard to distract myself from thoughts, horrid thoughts, about the life Clara must be living. I had my work, of course."

"I'm so sorry." Flynn gave Loveson time to collect himself as much as possible. "Isn't it amazing the quiet tragedies we all seem to suffer? It's a wonder we all don't try to be nicer to each other."

"Seven years later, when Callie was again hospitalized, when I had a sabbatical, I returned to Egypt to see if I could find Clara, find out anything about what happened to her. I spent almost a year there. I searched throughout the whole Middle East, Saudi Arabia, Iraq, Iran . . . I discovered nothing. She had been a pretty little thing. You may be surprised to know there were many such girls. And boys. Kidnapped from Europe, somewhere . . . I could do nothing for them."

"In your office, I found all those notes threatening you."

"I had them in a folder, in my locked filing cabinet."

"Why did you deny receiving them?"

"I guess I'm a little crazy, too." Loveson smoothed the light blanket on either side of him. "The notes were so childish. Cutouts from magazines. I knew they weren't from my colleagues. For one thing, they were not literate. Whoever was sending them to me was a person whose personal development had been arrested."

"Yes."

"Crazy of me, all these decades later. Some hopes never die." Loveson's eyes were wet. "I had the crazy notion they somehow might have been from Clara . . ."

Flynn said, "I think they were."

Loveson looked sharply at him.

"Tell me, how did you happen to hire Mrs. McElroy?"

"We needed someone. I was able to bring Callie home from the hospital again about three months ago. Perhaps I should leave her in the hospital permanently. I just like to have her with me, when it is possible. I, too, like to think of our lives before . . . the incident. Mrs. McElroy just showed up at the door, the first day we were home. A Saturday. Offered to work for us. What did you say about those notes possibly being from Clara?"

"You did not ask Mrs. McElroy for references?"

"She said the people at the hospital suggested she come work for us."

"You believed her."

"How otherwise would she have known about us? That we needed her."

"Professor Loveson, there is no Mrs. Enid McElroy."

Loveson's look was incredulous. "You mean I dreamed her? I'm not that crazy."

"We can find no record of her existence."

"You mean . . ."

Flynn waited without saying a word.

After a long time staring at the wall, Loveson said, "I've always thought how angry Clara must be at me, for not having been able to protect her. I was never very big. Never athletic. Those hoodlums left me unconscious on the road. I only became conscious in the hospital. How angry she must be that I was never able to find her. She wouldn't even know that I looked." After another long moment, Loveson looked at Flynn. "You think Mrs. McElroy is Clara, don't you?"

"She drives a small blue car, illegally, I guess. The magazines at your apartment have words and letters cut out of them. I'm pretty sure we'll be able to match them with the notes you received. Surely, your wife wasn't cutting out those notes and sending them to you."

"Surely not."

"The day before yesterday, while Gro—Richard was with you, you could not find your keys after Mrs. McElroy left. You didn't find them on your bureau, where you usually left them, until after Mrs. McElroy returned, the next morning."

Loveson said, "She used my keys to wreck my office and everything in it."

"Except the notes she herself sent you."

"What a horrible woman."

"What other motive could Mrs. McElroy have, if she is not Clara?"

"The poor, poor woman. She came to wreak her revenge on me. After the horrible life she must have led. Who can blame her?"

"She never gave you a chance to explain."

"Oh, explanations would have done no good. She still thinks with the mind of a child. Her daddy couldn't protect her. Her daddy didn't find her, rescue her from all that terrible experience which was her growing up, her life. I can't blame her."

"She surely wasn't there to clean your apartment. Or cook. Or take very good care of Mrs. Loveson."

"She was there to destroy me. Where is she now? Did she show up this morning?"

"No. I don't think she will. I think she's gone. I strongly doubt we'll see her again. Or that she will continue to be a threat to you. I think she's done what she came to do. Besides all that, I think she thinks I am wise to her. When I asked her yesterday afternoon about her having been in Egypt, she flew out the door like a rat who found a snake in his nest."

"Are you looking for her?"

"Not yet."

"Inspector Flynn, may I ask you not to look for Mrs. McElroy?"

"I don't know with what we could charge her, anyway. We can't prove she tried to hit you with a car. Other people, I'm sure, janitors must have a key to your office. It wouldn't be hard to violate that lock. Sending you childish, threatening notes . . ."

"I never thought I'd ask this: Inspector Flynn, please do not look for Clara."

"All right."

"Obviously it's too late. There's nothing Callie and I can do for her now. She found us. Expressed her hatred for me as well as she could. Tried to destroy me. Perhaps believes she did. Let that be the end of it."

"As you wish."

After standing, Flynn lifted his light chair back against the wall. "Regarding that nonsense on the Net earlier this week—and, I might add, those supposedly witty, insulting telephone calls you've been getting—I'm quite sure all that will stop, too."

"Don Carver was the ringleader?"

"Why do you suspect Carver?"

"He doesn't see the real need for ideas. He thinks they're just playthings, one no better than another. He'll learn."

"Yes," Flynn agreed. "He'll learn."

NINETEEN

———◆———

After parking the car, Flynn noticed double parked in the street outside the Old Records Building on Craigie Lane a large, dark, very clean sedan trying not to look like a limousine.

The car's driver, having all the appearances of a retired policeman, was trying not to look like a chauffeur.

"Ah," Flynn said to himself. "Cocky must have ordered in pizza."

He found Cocky sitting in the chess alcove of his office with the President of Harvard University.

"Inspector Flynn!" The President rose to shake hands. "I'm so glad you arrive before I have to leave."

"Mr. President."

"I mentioned wanting to see your office." Hands on his hips, the President looked at the ancient, scarred wood floors, wood walls, the fireplace, high-beamed ceiling, the great arched window behind Flynn's desk overlooking Boston Harbor. "It's much nicer than my personal workroom. Bigger. Has more character."

"What it has in size it lacks in housekeeping," Flynn said.

"I had more trouble getting into your office than I did getting into Harvard. My driver had to vouch for me. Having retired policemen as drivers has proven eminently useful. Lieutenant Concannon gave me a cup of herb tea. Sleepy Time, was it?"

Cocky nodded.

"Ach," said Flynn. "You'll never make it through dinner."

"Won't be the first time," the President said. "I have the sort of job which teaches one how to sleep with one's eyes open, while smiling and nodding beguilingly. The lieutenant has been regaling me with stories as to how it is to walk the beat."

"All lies, I'm sure," Flynn said. "Sure, and don't the police have too much time to make up stories?"

The President said, "I do believe I missed my calling. And you two always have a chess game in progress?" He looked at the board. "Who's black?"

"I am black," said Flynn. "I've had such an easy week, my concentration level hasn't risen to the point of being able to give Cocky a good game."

"Inspector, Dean Wincomb called me a while ago. He tells me Assistant Professor Donald Carver resigned this morning. He understands he is leaving the university without recommendation."

"He's decided to go quietly, has he?"

"He put that rubbish about Louie on the Net, didn't he?"

"Yes."

"But he did not destroy Louie's office?"

"No."

"And is that all you have to tell me about that?"

"Dr. and Mrs. Loveson will need your help, the help of the university, special help, from here on in."

"I visited Louie in the hospital last night. He seems to be getting on all right. All things considered."

"Perhaps after he retires he could have some continuing association with the university? He has little else. Mrs. Loveson isn't well."

"Certainly. But isn't there a daughter somewhere?"

Flynn said, "Somewhere."

The President smiled. "I think I see everything clearly, Inspector." The President shook hands with him again. "Many thanks. I'm sure I'll be talking with John Roy Priddy soon."

"I observe," Flynn said, "your eyes being open is not a perfect indication of your being asleep."

The President laughed.

Walking toward the elevator, the President said more quietly to Flynn, "I wonder if you would mind taking a piece of advice from Harvard's President, Flynn?"

"I'd be very grateful for any advice you have to give me, sir."

The President stepped into the ancient, wrought-iron caged elevator. He pushed the Down button.

He turned to face Flynn still standing in the corridor.

The President of Harvard said, "Move your queen."

TWENTY

—◆—

"Number 2211, is it?" In his tuxedo, Flynn drove the marked Boston Police car slowly through the residential street.

Cocky was checking the house numbers with the car's spotlight.

"2211."

Flynn had dressed formally, entered the Policepersons' Ball in a downtown hotel, greeted various and divers police colleagues—including Captain Reagan who, for once, with all his brass buttons and gold braid, was properly dressed—sampled the hors d'oeuvres, and waited.

At eight forty-five Lieutenant Detective John Kurt, his wife, and three other couples entered the ballroom.

"Ach," Flynn muttered to himself. "Society arrives late, doesn't it? At least it's a help knowing sometimes where Society is."

Flynn left the ball.

"There it is," Cocky said, "2211."

Flynn pulled into the short driveway of the one-level brick house.

"You're parking in the driveway of the house you intend to break and enter?" Cocky asked.

"I'm sure the neighbors of Lieutenant Detective John Kurt are used to seeing a police car parked in his driveway. They'll think nothing of it."

"What if anyone happens to look out and notice one of the burglars is wearing black tie? This isn't a good enough neighborhood for such a gentleman burglar. I doubt there's a diamond-studded tiara within miles."

"It will just confirm their suspicion that we police are a stylish lot." Flynn lifted the camcorder from the car seat between them. "You're in uniform, after all."

Cocky said, "I should have worn my tennis whites."

It took Cocky less than three minutes to deactivate the burglar alarm.

It took Flynn less than a minute to pick the lock of the back door.

Flynn snapped on the kitchen lights.

"You're putting the lights on?" Cocky blinked around the freshly painted kitchen. "Why don't we put a sign out front saying 'This house is being burgled'?"

"It'd be more suspicious seeing a flashlight moving around inside a house than the lights fully on, wouldn't you say? Besides"—Flynn lifted the camcorder—"we need full light. Well, let's start in the master bedroom, shall we?"

First, Flynn videotaped close-ups and then wide shots of photographs of John Kurt and his wife he found on their bedroom bureau. Then he panned their bedroom, their bathroom. While Cocky opened and closed their closet doors, Flynn shot their interiors.

After filming a neat guest bedroom, they moved back along the corridor to film the living room, kitchen, dining areas.

"The Kurts are remarkable housekeepers," Flynn commented. "House-proud, to use a German expression."

Cocky said, "Strange that such a good-looking, healthy young couple have no children."

"I suspect they are otherwise directed," Flynn said. "Did you notice the BMW in the back of the driveway?"

"Registered to Mrs. Kurt," Cocky said. "Anne Kurt. She's a primary school teacher."

"Expensive transportation for a primary school teacher. Do you wonder what it's meant to express?"

After videotaping the main floor of the house, they returned to the kitchen.

"Well," Flynn said. "We've established where we are. And so far found nothing. Will our luck hold?"

Cocky opened and closed a door to a broom closet. "This house must have a basement."

"Yes."

The second door he opened led to the basement steps.

In the basement, Flynn filmed the heating-cooling system, the washer and drier, the neatly stacked suitcases, the clean collection of lawn mower, rake, snow shovel, the floor-to-ceiling wine rack.

Cocky looked at two bottles of wine. "BMW tastes in wine, too."

"Cocky, old son." Not filming, Flynn was just looking around. "The ceiling is square."

"So's the floor," Cocky said.

"We're in a rectangular house."

"Yes." Cocky looked at all four corners of the room. "A half basement?"

"Half a basement, more like it."

"There's no way out. No door."

"Fiddle with that wine rack, if you will. That being the only object obscuring the wall in this subterranean world of Kurt."

Cocky removed the wine bottles from the left-hand side of the rack, waist high. "A regular doorknob." Cocky chuckled. "How clever!"

The wine rack swung open.

He entered the next room.

He switched on the light.

He said, "Oh, damn."

Flynn followed him with the camera.

Viewing through the camera, Flynn said, "Dear, dear. We found what we didn't want to find."

He filmed the huge Nazi swastika flag on the wall; the framed photographs of Hitler, Goebbels, Göring, and three other men he did not recognize, each of the three in a strange costume undoubtedly meant to be a uniform; the computer table, computer, and printer; the six metal chairs scattered in the room, another six folded against the wall.

He also filmed a large print hanging on the back wall.

On the right of the painting was a sunlit rural area, red barns and a white steeple in green rolling hills.

On the left side of the painting was a dark, urban area, squalid streets, decrepit redbrick buildings, windows smashed The tallest building, the top obscured by dirty clouds, had a Star of David on it.

In the middle of the painting, beautiful, muscular men and women marched from the rural area to the urban area. In their left hands the men carried assault weapons; the women, brooms.

The biggest figure was a blond man in the center of the painting, leading them, his right fist raised to the sky.

Flynn lowered the camera. "Oh, dear."

He felt so sad.

From across the room, Cocky said, "A sizable gun collection. Twelve assault rifles. Twelve forty-fives. Eight—"

"All right!" Flynn snapped angrily. "But is any of this actually illegal?"

"This is." Cocky was facing Flynn.

Between them was a chest-high concrete wall.

Flynn walked around the end of the wall.

On Cocky's side of the wall was a concrete work counter.

And on the counter were five bombs.

"Ah," said Flynn. "It's illegal to make bombs in a residential neighborhood?"

"Usually against zoning laws." Cocky laughed. "Of course it is."

As Flynn filmed the small bombs precisely spaced on the counter, Cocky commented: "These four essentially are ready for detonation. This last explosive device, as you can see, is a work in progress."

After filming, Flynn heaved a great sigh. "All right. Let's go upstairs and call Captain Reagan's personal communicator. He has it at the Policepersons' Ball with him. Tell him we found what we hoped not to find. Let's get out of here before a heavy truck goes by and sets one of these darlings off. Leave the lights on, Cocky. Lights will make the clean-up squad feel safer."

———

"Ha!" Flynn chortled. "Checkmate!"

Cocky sat back in his chair. "I suspect you had help, Flynn. Ever since you finally moved your queen—"

"Ah, a man is nothin' at all, Cocky, without a little help from his friends. Surely you know that."

"Who helped you?"

The television facing the old leather couch driveled on. A canned audience was finding something about a pregnant fifty-seven-year-old woman uncannily funny.

"Hark," said Flynn. "I hear the elevator. The man approaches."

Lieutenant Kurt entered the office closely followed by his wife. He looked around the big room.

Flynn and Cocky were on the couch, apparently watching the television.

"Flynn?" Kurt looked through the office's dark spots. "Inspector Flynn?"

"Ah, Lieutenant Kurt!" Flynn rose as if he had not known Kurt was there. "And Mrs. Kurt! How very nice of you both to come."

"Captain Reagan ordered me to report to you here." There was more contempt in Kurt's diction than curiosity. "Immediately."

"Yes, he did," Flynn said agreeably.

"In the middle of the Policepersons' Ball," Anne added.

Especially in his tuxedo did Kurt look handsome and physically fit. Tall, his shoulders were wide, his chest deep, his waist slim.

Flynn turned on the light over his desk. "Lieutenant Concannon and I have been looking at your remarkable conviction record, Lieutenant Kurt. Come, and look at it yourself, the way it's presented here."

Looking down at the desk, a slight smile played on Kurt's face.

"Isn't that remarkable?" Flynn asked Anne.

She nodded, blankly.

Forcefully, Kurt asked, "Why was I ordered here?"

"In the middle of the night," his wife added.

"You don't see anything remarkable about this presentation of your conviction record, Lieutenant? Nothing unusual?"

Cocky said, "Statistically impossible?"

"No."

"Lieutenant Concannon and I just wanted to point out to you how extraordinary your conviction record is." Flynn started back toward the couch. "Instead of your kickin' around the dance floor, we thought you'd rather kick back with us. Sit and watch a bit of television with Lieutenant Concannon and me. Relax, after your great labors." Flynn sat on the divan. "Pull up a pew, you two. This program is hilarious. It suggests the variety of human nature, it does."

Kurt and his wife stood behind the divan.

Impatiently, Kurt said, "What the hell is this about? I've heard of you, Flynn. 'Reluctant' Flynn. A damned eccentric, ignorant of police matters, the law . . ."

"I've got it!" Cocky said. "The President of Harvard!"

That confused Kurt.

Cocky pressed the videotape button.

On the screen appeared first a beautiful photograph of Anne Kurt, then one of John Kurt, then one of them together, then a panning shot of their bedroom.

Anne gasped.

"I compliment you on your housekeeping, Mrs. Kurt," Flynn said over his shoulder. "Your house is immaculate throughout!"

"Jack! Our bedroom!"

Kurt shouted, "What's this about, Flynn?"

"Sure, and you could eat ice cream off your kitchen floor, so clean it is!"

"Good taste in wines, too." Cocky fast-forwarded the tape.

"That's right, Cocky. Speed it up. Our guests are familiar with their own home."

Cocky slowed the tape to show him opening the door concealed as a wine rack in the Kurts' basement.

"Oh, God!" Anne gripped her husband's arm. "Jack!"

Kurt's hands were gripping the back of the couch.

On the screen, the camera was entering the lit, hidden room. The Nazi swastika flag came to fill the screen.

Overvoice, Flynn was saying, "Dear, dear. We found what we didn't want to find."

"Son of a bitch!" Kurt shouted. "What right did you have to enter my house?"

Flynn handed Kurt a piece of paper over the back of the couch. "This warrant."

Kurt looked at it. "Goldston. Judge Goldston. I might have known."

He dropped the warrant on the couch.

"You'd never have known about the warrant, if we had found nothing."

The five bombs appeared on-screen.

Overvoice, Cocky said, "These four essentially are ready for detonation. This last explosive device, as you can see, is a work in progress."

Flynn stood up. "Show's over." He smiled at Anne. "Surely, parts of this tape can be readied for submission to *House Pretty* magazine, or whatever it's called, without any editing at all."

Beneath his tuxedo jacket, Kurt's shoulders were visibly flexed.

Tight-jawed, Kurt said to Flynn, "What can you do?"

Anne pulled her husband's arm. "Jack! Let's get out of here! This is crazy. This crazy place. This can't be serious."

"Me? What can I do?" Flynn answered, "Nothing. I'm afraid your problem is educational, Lieutenant Kurt." He lit his pipe. "There is nothing I can do to improve your education at this point. At least, not all in this night."

Anne said, "In fact, my husband has done nothing wrong."

"He has a right to his opinions," Cocky said. "But not to run an unlicensed bomb factory."

Flynn pointed his pipe stem at the display on his desk. "Your husband has been using his position on the Boston Police force with bias."

Looking up over the back of the couch at Anne, Cocky

said, "The bombs you have in your basement, lady, could blow up half the town!"

"Falsifying evidence . . ." Flynn watched them both carefully.

"Jack. Jack!" She tugged her husband's arm. "Come on. Let's get out of here. Let's go home."

Flynn glanced at the clock on the mantel. "I expect the bomb squad is still there, Anne. At your pretty home. Captain Reagan and I thought we would delay you—and your friends—to avoid an unfortunate accident, being as we are, all police together."

"'Accident,'" Cocky snorted. "The resistance of you and your friends, Kurt, could blow up all your neighbors, women, children, dogs, cats, and canaries lost in the trees."

Kurt looked at Cocky. "You two can't keep me here. I'm black belt—"

"Ah, blather," said Flynn. "I keep telling you, lad. You've got a bad educational problem. You don't know blather from bombast."

Flynn had heard the elevator clank down to the first floor, then rise again.

He was expecting people in blue uniforms to enter the office, to arrest Boston Police Lieutenant Detective John Kurt and carry him off to the hoosegow.

Instead, it was Grover, alone, who entered the office.

He carried on both forearms a stack of magazines. The stack reached nearly to his chin.

Grover blinked in the office's pools of light. "You here?" he asked Flynn.

"All present," Flynn said. "The ball is over. At least, for some of us."

An odd glaze had come over Kurt's eyes.

Standing in the office doorway, burdened with the stack of magazines on his arms, Grover said, "A male nurse from Human Services finally arrived at the Lovesons' apartment. He says he's going to file a complaint about me, a cop taking care of a sick old woman overnight. I called Human Services early this afternoon. Finally he showed up at nearly midnight."

Kurt turned on his heel.

With determination he started to walk toward the door.

His wife followed him closely, as if tethered to him.

Seeing Kurt marching toward him, fists clenched at his sides, Grover continued uneasily. "I thought I had better rescue these magazines. You said you absolutely want them."

Kurt stopped in front of Grover in the doorway.

Following her husband so closely, blindly, Anne Kurt bumped into him.

Kurt said, "You going to try to stop me from going through that door, Whelan?"

Clearly, Grover had no idea what he was going to do.

He had no idea what was going on.

Bending his knees properly, Grover leaned over to put the stack of magazines on the floor.

Apparently, his head close to the floor, Grover saw Kurt brace his feet on the floor.

And, apparently, thinking he was about to be clobbered, instinctively Grover raised his left forearm over his head.

Knees bent, head down, clearly intending only to stand back, get away from Kurt, Grover sprang up from the floor like a powerful spring unsprung.

Without looking, he raised his left arm as he sprang, in an effort to keep his balance.

The cast on Grover's left wrist connected with Kurt's nose with enormous, unintended kinetic energy.

Kurt's nose was smashed into his head.

Falling backward, Kurt knocked over his wife.

"Good lad, Grover!" Flynn shouted from across the room. "You got the both of them with one blow!"

In her evening gown, Anne Kurt lay spraddled on the floor. Her unconscious husband was docked between her legs. His nose bled profusely on her organdy gown.

In flight-or-fight stance, legs apart, fists and arms raised, still expecting to be attacked, Grover stared at the formally dressed couple on the floor.

"Did I do that?"

Pinned by the weight of her husband's heavy shoulders and chest on her torso, Anne was trying to wriggle out from under him. Simultaneously, she was trying to wipe the blood pouring from his nose off her party dress.

Kurt was totally coldcocked.

Grover looked at Flynn. "I did that?"

"Indeed you did, Grover. Indeed you did. Well done! There hasn't been a better use of a cast since Branagh's *As You Like It*!"

TWENTY-ONE

Late the next afternoon, Flynn left his house to go for a walk by himself.

He had spent that Saturday midday attending Jenny's victorious swim meet. For the fifty-eleventh time, Flynn had marveled at how otherwise apparently reasonable people, parents, coaches, other fans at a swim meet, could cheer, holler, scream, stamp their feet encouragingly, shout advice at competing teenagers whose heads were underwater.

All that noise in a confined, tile environment had left Flynn's ears ringing.

A mile from home, ringing the doorbell of Anthony Capriano's condominium, Flynn heard through the door a recording of a Paganini violin concerto being turned off.

The door opened.

"Mr. Flynn?"

Flynn had telephoned ahead, asked if a visit from him would be welcome that afternoon.

Through the open door, Flynn's nostrils instantly were assaulted by the smells of Italian cooking.

"Mr. Capriano."

The smile in the strong old face was wonderful. "You don't know people call me Mr. Anthony?"

They shook hands as Flynn stepped through the door.

"Let me help you with your coat."

At age seventy-nine, Anthony Capriano seemed far more physically fit than his two sons, Tony and William. His shoulders were broad and still full. His arms looked like they could still heft half a cow without strain.

His stomach was a great deal flatter than his sons'.

His eyes were as bright and lively as his grandson's.

While Mr. Anthony was hanging up Flynn's coat in a hall closet, Flynn looked around the living room.

As a widower, Mr. Anthony had found a convenient place to live, however anachronistic it was.

A glass window running along one whole wall threw too much light on the heavy, dark furniture and rugs of the room. It caused the dozens of framed photographs in the room to glare from almost every angle.

Clearly this was the living room of a widower who had given up his family home, but not much of his family furniture: a mahogany gate-legged table where probably babies' diapers had been changed and family parties held, a massive couch where guests had slept and teenagers sprawled, stuffed armchairs where he and his wife doubtlessly had sat and loved and argued and laughed and cried and ruled the family.

Certainly Mr. Anthony had not given up many framed photographs of the family. They seemed to fill every inch of wall, every table surface.

There were wedding photographs of Mr. Anthony and

his wife, photos of their parents, of their children, Tony and William and a third son as toddlers in Easter suits, in First Communion suits, in Little League Baseball uniforms, football helmets, military uniforms; pictures of their weddings and children; pictures of cars then new, the interior of the butcher shop through the years.

"It is proper and correct that you should visit me, Mr. Flynn." At a heavy buffet table, Mr. Anthony poured out two generous glasses of red wine. "I hope the smell of my cooking does not bother you."

"I'm enjoying it."

"Good!" Mr. Anthony placed Flynn's glass of wine on a table beside the chair he expected Flynn to use. "I am expecting a very young couple for dinner." He sat in a heavy, brown, upholstered chair which probably had been his personal chair most of his adult life. "My grandson, Billy." Smiling again, he showed rows of apparently perfect teeth. "And your wonderful daughter, Jenny." He saluted Flynn with his wineglass. "I compliment you and Mrs. Flynn on your daughter."

"And I you on your grandson." Flynn raised his glass, then took a taste of his wine.

Savoring his red wine, Mr. Anthony said, "Jenny promised to bring her violin with her tonight, play for me again. I enjoy her playing, of course. But watching her face while she plays is an even greater treat. She concentrates so. Wrinkles her nose. Her blue eyes grow huge when she is going through a difficult passage. When she's done with a difficult passage, she sticks out her lower lip and tries to blow her hair off her damp forehead."

Flynn laughed. "I didn't realize you know Jenny so well."

"Oh, yes. Billy has brought her here often. I chide her since I discovered she knows nothing of Paganini. Before you arrived I was dusting off some recordings of Paganini, to play for her while we eat."

"My fault, I'm afraid. I've been thinking Paganini too difficult for her. Perhaps not."

"Italian. You knew she was coming here tonight?"

"Not really. I knew she was to dine with the Capriano family. I thought she meant Billy's parents."

"Just the three of us. I met Jenny at a family dinner at my son's house, of course. Billy usually stops in to see me three or four times a week. You don't like your wine? Good Italian red wine?"

"It's very good. I never drink."

Mr. Anthony nodded. "Then you were good to join an old man in our mutual salute." He pronounced salute in Italian. "I understand people find my manners a little old-fashioned. Jenny seems to respect them."

"Of course."

Mr. Anthony sipped his wine. "I hope I'm not wrong. You are here as Jenny's father, not as an inspector of police?"

"More than either," Flynn answered, "I'm here as a seeker after truth and wisdom."

Mr. Anthony's eyebrows rose in surprise. "Oh?"

"Tell me, please, why did you nail your grandson's ear to the tree?"

Mr. Anthony looked even more surprised. "You know about that?"

Flynn smiled.

"Of course! You must be the one who rescued Billy!"

"He didn't tell you?"

"No. He wouldn't. Obviously, I knew someone had rescued him."

"Last Sunday evening Jenny found Billy in the cemetery, his ear nailed to a tree. She came and got me. And tools."

"Did Billy tell you it was I who nailed his ear to the tree?"

"Absolutely not. He convinced me he was ready to rip his ear from the tree rather then tell me or Jenny who nailed him there."

"So?"

"When I realized only Thursday he was nailed to a tree in the Capriano family plot . . ."

"Yes." The rhythm of Mr. Anthony's speech became almost operatic. "Let him stand there, surrounded by the graves of his ancestors, his great-grandparents, his grandmother, the place where I will be buried, his father and mother. Let him consider his place in this world, in the Capriano family. Let him consider the standards, values by which we all have lived. Let him consider his disgrace in the face of family. Let him think about himself, make the decision right then and there as to what his standards and values are, whether he is a member of the Capriano family or not!"

"And rip his ear from the tree?"

Mr. Anthony shrugged. "Or live with us all forever with his shame."

"Shame for what? What disgrace? What did Billy do?"

Mr. Anthony's speech shifted from the lyrical to the straight dramatic. Eyes wide he shouted: "He wrestled with a girl!"

He shouted so loudly Flynn's ears were stunned.

"What?"

"The Thursday before! At school! At a wrestling match with another school! I was not there! Billy wrestled with a girl! I had to read it in the newspaper. William Capriano, Jr., physically wrestled with a girl!"

"Ah."

"I called him to come over immediately on the Sunday afternoon I read it. I hit him with the newspaper! I said, 'What's this? My grandson wrestling with a girl?' He said he felt bad about it. That he hadn't wanted to do it. He pleaded with his coach not to make him wrestle with a girl. Some nonsense about her being a member of the other school's team. That he had to wrestle a girl, or get off his team! Think of that! Our schools teach boys to fight with girls! I hit him again with the newspaper. I said, 'You're a Capriano! Caprianos do not beat up women! Not under any circumstances! You should have refused! Absolutely!' He said he couldn't refuse. 'Rules,' he said. I said, 'You obey Capriano rules! You should have sent your coach to me! I'll wrestle with him! Men do not beat up women!' I dragged him by his ear to where his family is buried and nailed his ear to a tree before their graves and said, 'There! Now you think about that!'"

Flynn was thinking.

Professor Louis Loveson, in trying to explain culturally why a boy had had his ear nailed to a tree, had said, "I suspect he did something unmanly."

Indeed he had.

Unmanly in his grandfather's eyes.

Flynn said, mildly, "These days girls are on school wrestling teams. Boys, girls—"

"Never!" Mr. Anthony shouted. "Greeks, Romans, invented wrestling. Boys wrestle boys. Men wrestle men!" He waggled his index finger like a windshield wiper gone berserk. "Never in history, never in anybody's culture, have boys wrestled girls! Have boys been taught, encouraged to fight with women!"

"Of course not."

Mr. Anthony went into the kitchen.

Flynn heard pot lids clashing.

"Look!" Mr. Anthony returned to the living room. "Men cook! Look!" He took his clean, folded handkerchief out of his pocket and threw it on the floor. Then he picked up his handkerchief. "Men can pick up around the house! I make my bed! Do my laundry! There is no shame in that! I helped my wife around the house. For years she worked with me in the store! She even cut meat. There was nothing unwomanly in that! We made love, made children! Never did I strike her! Never did I fight her! Never did I ever want to give her physical pain, make her feel she was my victim, physically or in any other way. Never did I beat her! We did not wrestle! We made love! That is what you do with a woman! Not beat her!"

He sat back down in his chair.

He rubbed his eyes with the strong fingers of one hand.

He said, "Men fight men. Men and women make love."

Flynn said, "Yes."

"Why did you free Billy from the tree?"

"He had time to think. What you wanted to happen to him in the cemetery did happen. I was convinced he would tear his own ear from the tree."

"Still . . ."

Flynn laughed. "I have a daughter, Mr. Anthony. She loves Billy's ear!"

Mr. Anthony began to chuckle. "She bought him an earring for the nail hole!" Looking at Flynn, he laughed out loud. "A gold earring!"

"Yes," laughed Flynn. "How can you buy one gold earring?"

"She must have bought two of them!" said Mr. Anthony.

"Good!" said Flynn. "Next time Billy does something unmanly, you can nail his other ear to a tree!"

"I will," Mr. Anthony said. Then he said, "I doubt he will."

"I do, too," Flynn said. "But if he does, for Jenny's sake, please make sure the nail holes match!"

Flynn rose to go.

Holding his coat for Flynn, Mr. Anthony said, "A lesson. I gave my grandson, Billy, a lesson. No matter what the world says for you to do, even orders you to do, you do what you know is right. Fighting with girls, beating them up, is not right. Even if she volunteers to be on other team. Billy knew that. Billy knew that from the family."

Flynn said, "From the Capriano family, anyway."

———

"Da! What are you doing here?"

Violin case gripped in one hand, Billy's hand gripped in

the other, Jenny found her father on the sidewalk outside Mr. Anthony's condominium.

"Visiting a friend."

In the misting dusk Jenny and Billy were straightly erect, happy-eyed, fresh-skinned, rosy-cheeked. They looked like they had been well exercised during that day; that they knew they were loved, respected, respected themselves; loved and respected each other.

Self-consciously, Billy stuck his hands in his jacket pockets. "My grandfather lives here."

Flynn said, "He's the friend."

"You know my grandfather?"

"We just met," Flynn said. "Became friends."

Billy frowned. "You didn't talk about—"

"Yes. Your grandfather nailed your ear to the tree because you wrestled a girl."

Jenny gasped. "Billy! Your grandfather—"

"Yeah." Billy watched the toe of his sneakered foot clean out a crack in the sidewalk. "He was right. I was ashamed to wrestle a girl. I didn't want to. I was afraid of . . . you know."

Flynn said, "I know."

"Coach said I had to. Or get off the team. Well . . ." He blushed. "What I was afraid would happen did happen. You know?"

"Yes," Flynn said.

"I was embarrassed. Ashamed and embarrassed. I had to finish her off quickly. It wasn't fair to her. I mean, as a wrestling competitor, you know? I felt stupid. Ashamed, embarrassed. I knew it was wrong. I wanted to stay on the wrestling team. I knew it wasn't right."

"Billy," protested Jenny. "You and I have wrestled together."

"Oh, no." Looking into Jenny's eyes, gently he put his fingertips on the back of her hand. "No, we haven't, Jenny."

Blushing, Jenny looked at her father. "No. We haven't."

"That's fine," Flynn said, a bit embarrassed himself. "That's all right."

"It's not right to beat up women," Billy said. "In any way. At any time. For any reason."

The silly gold earring dangling from the top of Billy's ear flashed in the streetlight.

Flynn said, "You youngsters go in to dinner now. It smells delicious. I'll talk to your coach Monday morning, Billy. I expect, if strongly enough urged, he can jiggle your match schedules sufficiently so this occurrence will not happen again."

"Oh, no," said Billy. "State law—"

On a misty sidewalk at dusk this Saturday, Inspector of the Boston Police Department Francis Xavier Flynn, No Name 13, said to his daughter, Jenny, and her boyfriend, Billy Capriano, as he walked away from them, "To hell with the law."

ABOUT THE AUTHOR

Gregory Mcdonald is the author of twenty-five books, including eleven Fletch novels and four Flynn mysteries. He has twice won the Mystery Writers of America's prestigious Edgar Allan Poe Award for Best Mystery Novel, and was the first author to win for both a novel and its sequel. He lives in Tennessee.